Dance
for Me

USA Today Bestselling Author
J.C. VALENTINE

Dance for Me
Forbidden Series Book One
by J.C. Valentine

Dance for Me by J.C. Valentine
Copyright © 2015 by J.C. Valentine
Cover design by Arijana Karčić, Cover It! Designs
Edited by Mitzi Carroll.

respective holders. The author acknowledges the trademark status in this work of fiction. The publications and use of these trademarks is not authorized, associated with, or sponsored by the trademark owners.

Acknowledgements

I usually don't make many changes to these things because, well, why mess with perfection?

To my usual suspects:

My sister from another mother, Kim- You are the best! What has it been now, two years? I never could have imagined that I would be friends with such an amazing woman as you. You read everything I throw at you, you're my sounding board, and you help keep me sane. It is such a pleasure to have you as my assistant and I am truly blessed to call you my friend. You are the one who gave me the idea of a naughty professor. Brainstorming with you was so much fun and I had a blast writing this story. I hope it's everything you imagined it would be.

Mitzi- What can I say, except you're such a wonderful woman who is also an unexpected friend and gift in my life. I've said it before, and the same is true now: I love our talks, and I love your passion for books, especially mine *grins*. You rock!

My Valentines! You ladies rock my socks off. I love our little family and as always, I am confident in saying that you're the best team a girl could ask for. You all pimp so hard! Thank you!

To all the people that take the time to connect with me: Every message, every comment truly means the world to me. I read every one, so keep 'em coming!

To my readers: You're the best. You've stuck by me from the beginning, when I wasn't even sure anyone was paying attention. I am continually blown away by your enthusiasm for my stories and your endless support.

I could never forget my darling hubby. You're my inspiration behind all of these delectable men. You're my rock, my one true love. I love you!!

Books by
J.C. VALENTINE

Night Calls
Stranded
That First Kiss
Surrender to Love
Trust

Wayward Fighters
Knockout
Tapout

Blue Collar
Sweetest Temptations

One

Whoever said life was fair must not have been talking about me. Growing up, I was a dreamer. A little girl with raven black, bouncing pigtails who was convinced that Jude McIntyre, my second-grade crush, would one day realize that I was a girl instead of one of the boys. I dreamed he would one day set those mesmerizing ice blue eyes on me and the world would realign. He would sweep me into his arms and carry me off into the sunset and together we would live an amazing life with two-point-five kids.

But that was just a fairy tale, and fairy tales don't come true. At least, not for people like me.

By the time I turned eight, my world as I knew it had begun to collapse, and dreams like boys and marriage and kids had evaporated. The only concern I had was keeping Dad happy and praying to God to give us another good day.

It was two weeks before my eighth birthday that the doctor diagnosed my mother with an inoperable brain tumor. He gave her two years. She was gone less than six months later.

Nothing mattered after that except getting from one day to the next. If Jude McIntyre or any other boys ever noticed my existence, I didn't know it. I was too busy making sure the man, who used to carry me around on his shoulders and told silly jokes at the dinner table, didn't waste away. After Mom had died, Dad became a shell. He went to work only because there were bills to pay. He only ate out of habit, and the blank stare, that never seemed to go away, made me wonder if he even tasted what I laid in front of him.

Dad passed away of natural causes shortly after my eighteenth birthday.

I say it was a broken heart.

He held on only long enough to make sure I made it into adulthood, and then he let it all go to be with Mom. I can't say I blame him. I miss her, too. I miss them both. But now isn't the time for crying. What's done is done. Now, my only concern is carving a path through this minefield called life, and I do that the only way I know how.

The floor-to-ceiling curtains hide my figure from curious eyes as my song of choice filters through the speakers, but I can feel them— touching, craving, yearning... *For me.*

This feeling used to scare me shitless. The vulnerability. The exposure. But all of that is long gone. Now, all I feel is the rush.

Being a stripper wasn't my life's ambition. Far from it. If my parents were looking down on me now, I don't think they'd be very proud of what their daughter has become, but this job is the key to my survival. Waiting tables doesn't pay much, but taking off my clothes means the difference between paying the bills and living on the streets. Student housing isn't cheap, no matter how you slice it. As a bonus, with all the tips I've saved up, I will have paid my tuition in full by the time I'm finished with my degree.

Right now, stripping is the solution I've chosen, because nothing else makes sense. And, if I'm being honest, I kind of like it.

The sensual beat of Porcelain and the Tramp's "I feel perfect" signal the show is about to begin. Standing with my feet slightly apart, I watch the dark curtains part in the middle. For one prolonged moment, I remain shrouded in a blanket of darkness. Then, as the lyrics take over, the ruby spotlight exposes me, and my feet begin to move. As I walk slowly forward, kicking my long legs out in front of me, I'm unable to see my audience, but I can feel them.

This is how I do what I do. I am shy by nature, but I learned early on that if I can block out the eyes watching me, my love of dancing is free to take over. At the end of the stage, I grasp the gleaming silver pole and twist, pressing my back into it. The shadowed figures watching my every move hover in the darkness just beyond my reach, urging me on.

Slowly, I slide down the length of the metal bar, my legs bending at the knee and opening wide, exposing the glittering gold strip that serves as a barrier between their eyes and the most intimate part of me.

There is something about taking my clothes off for strangers that I find exhilarating. It's the knowledge that all those eyes are focused on me, on every movement, no matter how small, and that I affect them. It gives me a sense of control, of power. I push these men to the brink, testing the limits of their willpower, and the only thing they can do is watch.

And give me their money.

Dropping to my knees, I crawl across the stage. Encased in stretchy gold fabric, my breasts sway with each movement, creating a hypnotizing effect. Men can't get enough of breasts, and thankfully, I have plenty to flaunt.

A few feet from the end of the stage, when I have reached as far as I am willing to go, I stretch my arms across the hard, cool surface, like a cat. Making eye contact with the darkness, I'm aware that whoever is on the other side is meeting my gaze with strained desire. Easing onto my back, I lift my hands overhead and stretch my long legs into the air, opening them wide, and then closing them again. The arch of my back presses my breasts toward the ceiling. Imagining what I must look like—nearly naked, needy and wanting, my body moving and arching, calling for my love to take me here, now—makes me feel edgy and wanton. As if the little clothing I wear is too much, threatening to smother me.

I'm not an exhibitionist, but there are times like this that an almost overpowering need to push past my own limits threatens to consume me. It takes everything I have to pull back.

Rotating onto my stomach, I push up onto my knees, reach for the pole again, and pull myself up. With both hands, I lift myself from the floor and bring both of my legs up, swinging in a full circle. Bills flutter to the stage, and I feel my smile inch up, slow and seductive.

It is then that I feel *Him*.

I'd noticed Him my first night on the job about five months ago before I learned the importance of lighting. He stuck to the perimeter of the room, choosing the same table in the same dark corner every time. From what I could tell, he had long legs, he was tall and had dark, almost midnight hair. The air of importance that cloaked Him made me peg Him as a professional. Although he alternated between jeans and slacks, polos and button-downs, I remember thinking he looked like the kind of guy who should be wearing business suits—sharp, expensive, and tailored.

He isn't a regular by any stretch, but he's definitely a creature of habit. I'd only seen him a total of four times before I began plunging the room into darkness—and I've only felt his presence a handful since—but I never miss the short glass, two-fingers, neat. My stomach flutters remembering those dark, penetrating eyes focused solely on me, glued to my every move, every sway, reading my body like a book. I'd never been more turned on in my life than the day I laid eyes on him—a perfect stranger.

He is the reason I now perform under the cover of darkness. I know if I had to see those eyes watching me, I'd never make it through my performance without combusting.

Times like this, I wished for a private dance. A chance to get up close and personal with my mystery man, but not knowing only added to the experience.

Asking around about Him isn't an option. I've made it a point not to get close to the personnel. This isn't the type of place I want to make friends. I came to dance, make a quick buck, and go home. No, the people I choose to associate myself with are classy, intelligent, and would never be caught dead in a place like this. If anyone found out what I did for a living… I'm not sure what would happen, but I'm not willing to find out.

Sensing Him watching me, I feel a familiar thrill tickling my insides. True heat spreads through my limbs, pooling in my stomach and lower as I imagine those dark eyes. What is He thinking right now? Is He imagining me, like I'm imagining him, his hands on my hips, his hot mouth tasting my skin? Pressing my breasts to the pole, I draw my focus inward, silently devoting this dance to Him.

I've built up a lot of strength since I began dancing, and I use that power now to pull myself up the pole. Wrapping my legs around it, I lock my feet at the ankles and release my hands. Arching back, my body folds over, until I hang upside down with only my legs to hold me. With my long black hair sweeping the floor, the gentle curve of my throat exposed, and gravity drawing my breasts up to full, round mounds, the effect is nothing short of erotic. When I allow my hands to touch my fevered skin, I imagine they are his, and find myself hoping he is doing the same.

When the dance is over, I collect the cash and hurry off-stage just as the lights come up. Just before I duck through the curtains, I glance toward the corner. My breath is lost the instant those dark pools of black meet mine. My feet continue to carry me to safety, but I don't miss the seductive curve of his lips, nor the promising wink he sends me.

Two

I rap my knuckles on the door twice—two quick, rapid taps. It's our signal. Sometimes, I pretend that this is a little game we play to keep the intimacy alive, but the reality of it is that the man behind the door is more concerned with secrecy. It doesn't take a lot of imagination to guess why.

I don't know what possessed me to accept His invitation, but I've been coming here every second Thursday and every first Sunday for months, ever since he'd taken an interest in my routine. He knows nothing about me, and I know nothing about Him, except that he likes control, an occasional glass of scotch, and he fucks like a god.

If I had to explain it, it'd sound crazy. The truth is, I have no idea how I got here. It just happened one day, and it keeps happening. And I'm not inclined to stop anytime soon.

He could be married. He could have kids. He could be a drug smuggler. I have no way of knowing, but I know that the few hours I spend in his bed are some of the best, most exhilarating moments of my life. At least when I am old and gray, I'll be able to say I had lived.

The door cracks open revealing nothing but darkness and I am sucked inside by a strong, unyielding arm. A squeak of excitement leaves me as I am whirled around and my back is slammed up against the door.

Hard, punishing lips crash down on mine, and a hot, wet tongue forces its way past my teeth. I moan shamelessly as my purse drops to the floor and my hands find the short fine hair that I know to be as black as the midnight sky.

My mystery man is always hungry after watching me dance.

Ripping the button on my jeans free, he plunges his hand into my panties and groans as his fingers part my moist folds. "Jesus fucking Christ. Always so wet," he mutters as he nips my jaw, and then begins moving down my neck.

I am always ready for this, for Him. Maybe it's because he's my only source of sexual release besides my fingers since I broke it off with Eli last semester, or because he is so talented in the sack. But the truth of the matter is that a part of me gets off on the mystery. Our sex is just that—sex. It's wild and dirty and passionate and *honest*. Strip away the mystery, and you lose all of that. Maybe not right away, but one day.

Relationships almost always have an expiration date. I'm not naive enough to think our arrangement doesn't, but at least I know I won't lose anything in the process. When my mystery guy gets bored, I figure I simply won't see him again.

Right, I should be concentrating on what he is doing to me now. We only have so much time together, and I don't want to miss a second.

I feel Him lowering down to his knees, and I kick out of my shoes. I luxuriate in the feel of smooth, strong hands sliding patiently down my sides to my thighs, taking my jeans with them. My pants are then tugged free from my ankles, and they land somewhere in the room with a heavy plop. My panties follow them, and in an instant, I feel the magical heat of his mouth cover me.

Thrusting my fingers into his hair, I hold Him to me as he sucks my clit between his lips and feasts. He loves this. It's always the first place he attacks, and who am I to deny him that pleasure?

As his fingers push up inside me, my eyes cross and I tilt my pelvis higher, trying to get closer to that tricky little spot that needs his attention. But he isn't in the mood to play for long tonight. Must have been a long week. Of course, I'm only guessing because we never talk. About anything.

I don't even know his name, and he doesn't know mine. Like I said, we know virtually nothing about each other. Sex is all that connects us. Fantastic, life-altering sex.

I whimper in protest as his fingers and mouth leave me and he stands. In the slashes of light coming in through the window across the room overlooking the river, I can see that he is still dressed to thrill. He's wearing some kind of casual dark suit ensemble. I want to rip it off him and run my hands over all that honed muscle hidden beneath.

The light catches on his wolfish smile, the white of his teeth breaking up the dark, and he wipes his fingers over his mouth.

"Get naked and climb on the bed, ass in the air."

I shiver at the rough sound of his voice and I rush to do as he says. That voice haunts my dreams—dark and smooth, just like the liquor he drinks. I'll do anything he says, so long as he keeps talking.

With my butt up in the air, I look over my shoulder and watch as he removes his own clothing then climbs up behind me. Running the flat of his palm from the base of my spine to the nape of my neck, goosebumps break out all over my skin as he wraps a handful of my long, black hair around his fist and yanks my head back.

Gripping my hip in his other hand, he pulls me back against his straining erection. "I've missed this ass. Did you enjoy teasing me up on that stage?"

I scream as his hand comes down on me, my skin singing from the force of it. "Yes," I pant, pushing my hips up higher.

He smacks me again, and I swear my head spins. Like I said, we have passion between us. We know we aren't committed to each other, but he likes to tease me as though we are. It is the game we play.

"You like shaking those tits and this ass for all those sweaty, horny fucks, don't you? It gets you off."

"Yes," I groan as his hand slips between my legs, fingering my opening. If he didn't have such a tight hold on my hair, my head would have dropped to the bed already. My legs tremble beneath me as I feel the head of his cock stroke me from clit to ass.

"You feeling adventurous tonight, babe?"

I stiffen, knowing what he is asking of me. It is the only thing I haven't allowed him to do yet, and I'm uncertain if I am willing to try. It would just be another level to our dirty sexcapades, but I already moved up the ladder on his last visit when I let him fuck me against the window in broad daylight, for the entire city to see. If we don't pace ourselves, we'll run out of things to do to each other.

His low laughter pierces my thoughts. "You're thinking too hard. I'll make it easy on you, then. Tonight, no anal, but next time I want inside this tight hole." I am still reeling over his words when he shoves his way inside me, stretching me to capacity.

Sex with my mystery man is never nice. It is hard and fast and sometimes it leaves marks. For instance, I know my scalp is going to hurt tomorrow. He is riding me like a cowboy on a bronco, yanking and tugging on my hair so hard, it's difficult to concentrate on the hard cock between my legs. The hold he has on my hip is going to bruise, too. The force of his body slamming into mine is something I always relish, though. It's our connection. As long as he's buried inside me, I can pretend he's mine.

"Touch yourself," he demands, his words grating past his clenched teeth. He's getting close, and if I don't rub one out now, I'm going to lose out. What I learned early on is that he chooses when I get to orgasm and how. Sometimes he takes the extra time and care to work me out. Other times, like tonight, he plays then dives in. He doesn't wait. If I don't take care of it now, I'll be taking care of it later, alone in my bed.

The thing is, and what the romance books won't tell you, that sometimes it's friggin' impossible for a woman to get off, no matter how hard she tries. She can concentrate until she is blue in the face, or relax and let it come to her, but it's all a joke. Orgasms are like bobbing for apples. Sometimes you get one, but most of the time, you just ended up with wet hair, smeared makeup, and a backache.

Tonight, no matter how hard I try, I can't get there. So, I do what any woman would do who wants to please their man—I fake it.

"Ohhhhh ahhhhh," I moan into the bedding, really laying it on thick as I clench my inner walls around him. He thickens almost immediately, grunting as he comes inside me. Thank fuck for birth control and condoms. The man is so potent, it'd be stupid not to double up.

Dropping down on top of me, my arms collapse under his weight. The only sound in the room for several minutes after that is our sawing breaths and the pounding of my heartbeat in my ears as I struggle for adequate oxygen.

Finally, the pressure leaves me as my mystery man rolls away. From out of nowhere, I hear the loud crack and my ass cheek burns accordingly. "Mother fuck!" I screech, no longer in my sex-hazed delirium. There is no buffer to ease the sting this time. Shooting off the bed, I grab my cheek and send him a death glare.

His smirk is both an act of defiance, and a challenge. "Remember that next time you decide to fake it."

My mouth gapes open as he walks toward the bathroom. My indignation over being hit out of context and the shock of getting caught, burns away like fog on a sunny morning when I realize where he is going. Heat takes its place. "Need someone to wash your back?" Usually, he's good for at least two rounds—sometimes more. But he always takes time for a little aftercare. Those times are my favorite because it is the only time he's sweet. His behavior could almost fool me if I wasn't so accustomed to his ways.

"If you're offering. There are a few other places that could use some special attention, too."

A smile blossoms on my face as I push open the door and step inside. The water is already running in the shower, and the view of his naked ass, round and solid with muscle that rolls up to a smooth, toned back with broad shoulders, nearly sends me into a tizzy. A lesser woman would drop dead from the sight, it is so damn perfect. Me? Screw the washcloth. I plan to lick every inch of that skin.

He takes me twice more that night—once in the shower, filling my mouth with his cum, and the last in what is apparently his new favorite spot—in front of the window. Yes, my mystery man is a dirty boy, and I love it.

When the alarm on his phone goes off at five in the morning, just a few short hours after we fell asleep in each other's arms, I'm not ready to get up.

"Get up," he says, the words clipped. "I'm checking out in twenty."

Rubbing my eyes, I roll out of bed feeling as if I have one foot in reality and the other still in dreamland. "Why are you leaving so early? You usually get up at seven."

"I have to be somewhere."

"This early?" I'm immediately aware of my tone. He doesn't like complaining. A fact I'm reminded of as he glances over his shoulder— those harsh, onyx eyes threatening to level me if I don't shut my mouth fast.

Holding up my hands in surrender, I search for my clothes and begin dressing. "Forget I mentioned it. You want me out, I'm out."

I refuse to let his kicking me out hurt my feelings. Still, there's no denying the rejection stings a little.

Meeting me at the end of the bed, he places his hands on my shoulders, and I pause as I look up into his eyes. Is that regret I see?

"Don't let anyone see you when you go."

Nope. My mistake. A dick. That's what he is. And yet I keep coming back because I'm a stupid shit. "Of course. Same time next week?" I ask hopefully, hating myself for sounding so eager. If I had any self-respect, I'd tell him to fuck off.

"Unless something else comes up." That is always his answer. I don't know why I keep asking, because it never changes. He lowers his mouth to mine, and for a brief, fantastic moment, I am sucked back into the blissful state that he provides as our mouths fuse together.

I am breathless by the time he pulls away, and my head feels light as I slip from the room the same way I came in—silent and unnoticed.

Three

"Joe, wait up!"

I turn at the sound of my name and see Annie rushing toward me, her blonde hair bouncing around her shoulders. As usual, she's running late. Or, at least, she thinks she is. Annie is the type of person who thinks the clock is working against her the minute she walks out the door. In reality, she's always on time, if not early, for everything.

Stepping back so I'm not blocking the sidewalk, I wait for her, amused. A yard separates us, and I can tell from here by the pink in her cheeks and the intense look in her bold green eyes, that she's experiencing a freak-out moment. Beside me, Annie is petite, bordering on munchkin size and a perfect mixture of cute and drop-dead gorgeous. A bolt of shame strikes me briefly, because Annie would never be caught dead doing what I do for a living. She's too sweet, too pure. Combined with my late-night rendezvous, I feel soiled and used up standing beside her.

I shake the soul-damaging thought away as Annie reaches me and fall into step with her as she continues on. "You're really cutting it close," I tease her. "There's only twenty minutes left until class starts. We'll be lucky to get a front-row seat." Today I start my first art class, and I get the added bonus of sharing the experience with my best friend.

Annie shoots me a mock glower but increases her pace a fraction. "Not funny, Joe. I don't want to be late for this class. Everyone says the same thing: Professor Scott is a total ball-buster."

"Well, good thing we don't have any of those." I nudge her playfully, but I can see that Annie is in *The Zone*. Her playful side won't be free for at least another hour. "I'm surprised you haven't given yourself an ulcer already. Relax, would you? It's Art Comp. How hard could it be?"

As it turns out, those words would come back to haunt me.

We are the first students through the door. The room is set up amphitheater-style, with stadium- seating overlooking a half-circle floor where a small, functional desk and podium are set up. The florescent overhead lighting strains my eyes as I follow Annie across the floor to the first row, taking the seats positioned front and center, just the way she likes them. I prefer the back, as far away as one can get. This close, I'll be able to see the professor's nose hairs flutter while he talks.

As the class steadily files in, I lean into Annie and speak low enough that my voice won't carry. "So, how did it go with Jason last night? Did you get everything straightened out?"

Lately, she and her boyfriend have been having problems. She's been tight-lipped about it, but from what she's shared with me, they've been dating since the start of their freshman year at university and hit it off so well, they made plans to get married once they graduated. We are two weeks into the start of our first semester of senior year and it looks as though Jason is reconsidering his life plans. Distant, moody, and all-around jackass, I have a hard time understanding what she sees in the guy. He only comes around to get free ass, and then he's gone again, and I'm getting tired of seeing my friend mope around in his wake. The only reason I haven't said anything is because I know Annie is the type of person who needs to handle it in her own time and in her own way. This is precisely the reason I haven't settled down with anyone. If this is what I have to look forward to, I'll gladly stay single forever.

Even as the thought crosses my mind, a set of dark, penetrating eyes surface in my memory.

Rolling her eyes, Annie inhales deeply. "It didn't. As soon as we got to his dorm, his friends burst in and next thing I know, I'm sitting on a crowded couch on Frat Row watching him play beer pong and get wasted. I can't talk to him when he's like that." She looks at me, one eyebrow lifted. "And he's always like that these days."

The sadness radiating off her strikes me right in the chest. Annie is too good a person to be treated with such blatant disrespect. He's not the person she thinks he is. Jason doesn't deserve to have someone so loyal and loving. I am about to tell her this when the door bangs shut, resonating throughout the room.

"Roll call!" the heavy voice booms, reverberating off the walls.

My gaze lifts, and I experience an acute case of tunnel vision as I sit up straight. It takes my brain a few moments to catch up to what it is seeing, and when it does, I nearly hyperventilate.

Holy shit! Dear Lord in Heaven, this can't be happening. But it is. Professor Scott is my mystery man? And then, like a bolt of lightning, the heaviness of that realization strikes me and I realize, *Holy shit. Professor Scott is my mystery man.*

My gaze eats him up as it slowly slides down his trim body, starting from the top of his head and gliding appreciatively all the way down to his toes. He is scorching hot, so different from seeing him in the darkness of the club, or in the throes of passion. It's difficult for me to comprehend what is standing in front of me. His stark black hair, long enough to touch his shirt collar and curl up at the ends, is combed back off a broad forehead—it's the same—thick black brows, piercing charcoal eyes, slim nose, full lips, wide, unshaven jaw. Even the way his thick neck disappears beneath a powder blue button-down that tucks into a pair of crisp black slacks rings a bell. And I know from experience that the size of his polished black leather loafers is a precise indication of what's happening on the business end of things.

He is the total package, and for some reason, seeing him in this environment, I feel more connected to him than ever. We share a secret bond, one that I know I won't be able to ignore because as Professor Scott comes to stand in front of me, all I can think about now is how it feels to be impaled on his cock.

A low gurgle of laughter claims my attention before I get too far along with my fantasy, and I realize with sudden clarity that I am macking on my professor—*my lover*—who is standing only a foot away, those piercing black eyes fixated on me expectantly.

He smirks and my heart thuds against my ribcage. "Glad to see you've returned to us, Miss…?"

My face is burning, as surely as if someone is holding an open flame up to it, and I clear my throat. "Josephine Hart."

"Miss Hart," he purrs, and my insides twist at the sound of my name on his lips. "I'm assuming you weren't listening just now. We're doing roll call, and I have asked each member of the class to stand up and introduce themselves." His dark eyes hold mine, and despite his smile, I feel like a fly under a microscope. Even outside the bedroom, he's the same dominating man, always in control of the situation.

Professor Scott crosses his arms over his chest and tilts his head, and I realize he's having fun with this. "Guess who's next, Miss Hart."

My insides flip and flop. Public speaking is not my forte. It's my worst nightmare, actually. He'd know this if he ever bothered to get to know me.

"Me?" I squeak out, and with his silent nod, I rise on shaky legs. I hate him for forcing me to do this. How can I, someone who dances every night for a roomful of horny men, get a case of the shakes from merely talking in front of people? I don't understand it, but then again, not everything in life makes sense.

Focusing, I place all of my attention on him, drawing the strength I need from looking into those eyes that have held me steady for months. I've met his challenges before, and I'm determined to meet them again.

When I open my mouth to speak, I am surprised to hear my voice come out loud, clear, and steady. "My name is Josephine, but everyone calls me Joe. I grew up in Michigan, but moved here for school almost four years ago." With a large inhale, I begin to sit, but Professor Scott's voice stops me.

"And what degree are you pursuing?"

"Uh..." I stand back up, looking him in the eye. I can almost swear I saw a glint of something there as if he were getting some sort of satisfaction from my discomfort. Knowing him, he probably is. Folding my hands in front of me, I tell him, "Art. Art is my major."

"Are you looking to teach, or perform?"

"Perform?"

"Paint, draw, sculpt," he clarifies, and yeah, that subtle curve of his lips tells me he's enjoying this. Immediately, I take a mild dislike to this side of him, the one that has invaded my academic life, but at the same time my insides flutter. I shouldn't be getting turned on by this, and yet, I am.

"Painting and drawing," I answer firmly, and I know by the slight narrowing of his eyes that he approves of my answer. I shouldn't be happy about that.

He averts his gaze, freeing me from its mesmerizing effect, and I drop back into my chair. My heart continues to beat a mile a minute the rest of the hour. When our time is up, I stuff the handouts in my bag and grab Annie's wrist, hurrying her out of there as if my ass has caught fire. I don't slow down until we break out onto the campus and the warm morning sunlight hits my face.

"Who's the one running now?" Annie laughs as she releases herself from my grip and straightens the backpack hanging off her shoulder. She rotates it and grimaces. "Damn, I think you pulled my arm out of the socket. What was that back there? It was like he was focused on you. Have you had him before?"

Oh, I've had him all right. He's screwed me every way from Sunday. God, what a mess. Shaking my head, I rub my fingers over the ache blooming between my eyes. "No, this is my first class with him," I lie, "but what a jerk."

"Maybe he was teaching you a lesson for not paying attention," she says with a soft chuckle. "Whatever his problem is, I think you're in trouble. Either he's pegged you as trouble and is going to make your life hell or you're about to become teacher's pet."

My lip curls in distaste. "This is why I like to sit in the back." Maybe back there, I could have slipped under his radar the whole semester. Now, any hope of that is gone.

"Too late for that." With a quick hug, Annie waves as she breaks away in the direction of the science building. "Catch you later!"

I lift my hand in a limp wave and watch her go. Teacher's pet? A part of me is adverse to the idea, while another part of me is thinking of all the benefits that could come from it. We've never had sex bent over a desk before.

I'm getting ahead of myself. Nothing good can come of this, I tell myself. This man could fail me if I piss him off. My future is literally in his hands. Annie's right, though. It's too late to change anything now. The damage is done, and I need this class to graduate.

The thought is depressing, because I know he has me over the barrel, whether he realizes it or not. But I don't have time right now to stand around pondering my fate. I have four more hours to get through before I need to get ready for my shift at the club—*Mirage*. Putting the last hour behind me, I beat feet toward the English Department.

Four

The second my last class lets out I'm running for my car. Although the sun is still high and it's barely dinnertime, business at *Mirage* will be going strong as ever. There's always a steady flow of patrons when booze and naked bodies are on the menu.

Opening the trunk of my sun-bleached Toyota Camry, I toss the tote full of books and tonight's homework inside and exchange it for the black mesh bag that holds tonight's costume. A secret smile tugs at my lips as I picture it. For a brief moment, I allow myself to wonder if my mystery man—erm, *Professor Scott*—will show. If he does, I wonder what he'll think of the black, men's dress shirt and emerald green tie and thong

I'll be sporting. I wonder if he'll know that I'm wearing it for him.

As I maneuver through the parking lot, I catch sight of a familiar figure. He's standing in front of his own car, a shiny silver BMW, staring into the open hood with a look of consternation. He's stressed—I can see it in the firm set of his shoulders, and when he ruffles his dark hair and the frown grows deeper, I decide to pull over.

"Do you need some help?" I ask.

Professor Scott turns the full weight of those onyx eyes on me, and I shiver at the same time I flinch. He's not just stressed, he's pissed. In his hand, he grips his cell phone, and he lifts it, using it to point at the car. "The piece of shit won't start. It just keeps clicking," he growls.

When he recognizes me, his eyes narrow, and I hope it's just the glare of the sun that incites that reaction. Although, I know better.

"That's the first time I've ever heard of anyone refer to a BMW as a piece of shit," I quip, choosing to ignore his attitude. "Have you called anyone to come out and take a look at it?" The question is rhetorical. Obviously, if he's holding a phone, he would have already called someone.

"Of course," he snaps, giving me a look that says just how dumb he thinks the question is. "I pay almost two hundred a year and they tell me I have to wait an hour and forty-five minutes for the truck to arrive." He curses and the colorful language makes him somehow less a professor and more a person. More the man I am accustomed to.

This aggressive side reminds me of our last night together. Of the hard door abrading my back and the bruises he left behind on my thighs from where his fingers dug into my flesh—I feel a needy ache blooming between my thighs at the memory.

Staring at the open hood for a minute, I weigh all the options. If I stick around, I'll be late for work. If I go, I'm pretty sure that makes me a dick. Even though he ticked me off earlier when he kicked me out of his room and attempted to humiliate me in front of the entire class, I don't really get the impression he intends to be such a jackass. In fact, I think intense is just part of who he is. But he seems really freaking vulnerable right now. Maybe if I pull the Good Samaritan card, he'll let me lay low for the rest of the year.

With that little spark of hope simmering inside my head, I put the car in park and open the door. Professor Scott eyes me as I step out of the car as if it's the first time he's ever looked at me. That's absurd, since he's been watching me strip bare on a stage for months, and stripping me bare in private for nearly as long.

His is a slow perusal that starts at my face and works its way down to my feet and back up again. When he lingers on my chest longer than necessary, I glimpse that telltale spark that lets me know he likes what he sees.

I can't really fault him for it. I witness that same look in the men at the club every day. It's classic visceral attraction. The man likes what he sees, but he doesn't really know me, so that's where it ends.

Unless one of us decides otherwise.

Perhaps this newness is due to the change of scenery. Outside the walls of the club and the hotel, I'm a real person. Not some fantasy that he can fuck and set aside for later, like some kind of porcelain doll.

I stand a little taller feeling that infusion of power that usually only comes when I'm working the stage. "You said it clicks when you try to start it?"

"Yeah, it just clicks."

Brushing past him, I walk around to the driver's side and slide into the buttery black leather seat. This car is a luxury in both price and style, and I take a moment to commit the elaborate dashboard, hand stitched leather and chrome details to memory. Hell, even the little tree, that smells of men's cologne and hangs from his mirror, holds a special place in my head. Through the windshield, I see the professor blink hard and collect himself.

Right, time to teach him a little about who I am.

Although the car won't start, I try turning the ignition anyway so I can hear it for myself. It clicks once, and I watch for any signs of life from the dashboard. "Did it try to turn over the first time you attempted it?"

Crossing his arms over his chest, I can't help noticing how the material of his shirt pulls at the shoulders and around his biceps. *I had my hands on those last night*, I think, smiling to myself.

"The stereo lit up for a second, but it stopped working. Everything stopped working." His eyes narrow as he watches me get out. He tracks my movements, pivoting out of the way as I brush by him again to get a look under the hood. I know what he's thinking. What does this girl think she knows about fixing cars? The answer: more than him.

My '92 Toyota, a car that should last forever, is a lemon. The constant cost of repairs was eating up money as fast as I could make it, so I'd taught myself a few things. For instance, I know exactly what is happening to the professor's overpriced hunk of metal.

"Your starter is bound up," I say, looking over my shoulder at him.

His eyes widen in surprise, but then narrow into suspicion. "Let me guess, your dad or brother taught you a few things growing up."

Again, he'd know the answer to that if he'd ever taken the time to get to know me. I can see this is about to turn into a crash course for him.

"My dad's dead and I'm an only child," I say casually, though I can see, by the way he drops his arms down to his sides and takes a step back, that he is shocked and regretting that last statement. "What I know about cars, I taught myself. Your starter," I say, pointing at the car, "is shot. It's a relatively cheap fix, especially if you can do it yourself." I scan his fancy clothes critically. "But something tells me you're not up for the challenge."

He glances down at his clothes, as though trying to find something wrong with them. When he looks back at me, I see that my words have sparked something in him. Professor Scott reaches up to grip the top of the open hood. "And you are?" He treats me to the same look I gave him, eying my black tank top, white skinny jeans, and peep-toe pumps with contempt.

Smirking I say, "I don't mind getting a little dirt under my nails. Unfortunately, I just put a new coat of lacquer on them this week and I don't have time to redo them. What I can do, though, is drop you off if there's someplace you need to be."

I have to say, I am enjoying this. Turning the tables on someone who is always in control has got to sting. Payback for the sting I experienced when he so callously booted me from his hotel room.

I watch him closely, waiting patiently for his answer, but the clock is ticking. I can't afford to be late for work.

Professor Scott doesn't look very happy with his options, but thankfully, he doesn't take long to think them over. With a rough sigh, he slams the hood shut and retrieves his keys from the ignition. With very purposeful strides, he heads toward the passenger side of my car. "I'm meeting someone at the River Front Plaza. Do you know it?"

I should, considering it hosts the most upscale restaurant in the city, is a block away from the club, and he fucks me every other week at the hotel next door. Pointing this out to him, though, seems trivial. Of course, he already knows this.

Playing off the note of relief that it was on my way, the slice of disappointment that whoever he's meeting isn't me, and the excitement that I get to spend a little extra time with him, I climb behind the wheel and start the engine. "I'm familiar with the area," I say shortly.

Clipping his seatbelt, I notice that Professor Scott doesn't seem overly enthusiastic about the way his day is going. I, on the other hand, see a golden opportunity that has just fallen into my lap. As I ease up to the parking lot exit, I see the evening rush beginning to take hold, and at the first opportunity that presents itself, I shoot out into traffic.

"So business or pleasure?" I ask him as I speed up to beat a red light. We float through the busy intersection, just beating out the flash of the red light cameras that were installed last year. Beside me, the professor has a death grip on the door handle, and I chuckle to myself.

"What?" he says, his voice strained. I almost have to laugh, because this is the only time I have ever seen him outside of his comfort zone. Usually, he has all the control, and I am the one at his mercy. The feeling of power is heady.

Frankly, my driving is terrifying. I know this because Annie has told me many times, which is why whenever we go anywhere together, she drives. The problem isn't that I'm reckless, though. I'm aggressive. Not a lot of people can give up enough need for control to handle my driving, which is why it impresses me that he has been able to keep his comments to himself this long. But the sickly pallor suggests he might be on his way to an early heart attack, so I ease up on the pedal.

"Business or pleasure?" I repeat.

As the color returns to his face, Professor Scott pries his eyes from the road long enough to glance at me. "What do you mean?"

"Are you meeting a friend? Business associate? Your wife?"

"Pleasure, I guess."

I nod, pretending as if the information didn't just suck all the oxygen from my lungs. "So wife?"

He gives me an odd look, and I wonder if he's picked up on the strain in my voice. "You're my student, Josephine," he reprimands. "I'm not going to tell you that."

"That's fine," I say quickly, hardly fazed by his cool tone. "I already know you're not married. I'm going to guess girlfriend."

"And how do you know I'm not married?" he asks, turning to face me with one eyebrow arched.

Reaching over, I tap the third finger on his left hand. "No ring." It was the first thing I checked the night he'd handed me his business card and asked me to meet him outside the club. I may be many things, but I am not a home wrecker.

He looks away, out the window, and to my disappointment, the conversation ends before it begins. Pulling up to the restaurant, I take a moment to soak it in. I've never been inside, but the sheer size and grandeur of this building always takes my breath away.

I release a low, long whistle of appreciation as I lean over the steering wheel and peer up at the steel skyscraper. "Swanky."

Professor Scott chuckles softly and shakes his head. "That it is," he says, reaching for the door handle. "Thanks for the ride, Miss Hart. I owe you one. Enjoy the rest of your evening."

He's gone in seconds, and I pull away wondering just how he intends to pay me back. But as I enter through *Mirage's* back door, less than five minutes later, to the thick blanket of darkness and the pungent smell of perfumes, alcohol, and faint mildew that envelope me, the reality, that he was meeting with someone else, strikes me. Our time together has come to an end.

It shouldn't feel like someone has died, but I feel the familiar ache that followed my parents' passing like a knot forming in the center of my chest. Acid burns in my stomach and I have to remind myself that I knew this day was coming. I just didn't think it would be this hard to walk away.

"You're late, J." Kota, the owner of the club, enters the dressing room without knocking and leans his shoulder against the wall as he watches me change into my outfit.

His unwavering stare was creepy when I first signed on as one of his dancers, but as with most things in life, I got used to it. It helped to realize that Kota doesn't give two shits about how much skin is on display. He's been working the business long enough that one set of tits is the same as the next. He's more concerned with the bottom line.

"I had to help out a friend," I say vaguely, because less is more around here. The only thing

Kota or anyone else needs to know about me is what made it into my paperwork. "I'll work extra tables to make up for it before I go on."

"No tables," Kota says, his bald head shining as he shakes it. "I need you on the floor tonight."

I shrug and nod apathetically. All the girls have to trade off throughout the week, so since I'll be working the floor tonight it means someone will have to work the floor for me somewhere down the line. I guess this means I'll be changing my outfit tonight. "Who called off?"

"Christine. She's got the flu or some shit."

"Hope she isn't prego," I say with a laugh, but then I catch the scowl on Kota's face letting me know the joke wasn't appreciated, and it evaporates. Getting pregnant is the kiss of death. It's a guaranteed boot in the ass. Another incentive for me to keep it in my pants, so to speak.

Straightening his posture, Kota throws open the door, allowing the pounding music to flow inside. "Light a fire under it, Pussycat. It's going to be a busy night."

Five

Kota wasn't kidding when he said it was going to be busy. I've been racing around all night, and my body aches everywhere. After dropping drinks off at my last table, I tuck my tray behind the bar and wave my hand overhead to gain Kota's attention.

"I'm taking my break!" I shout, and when he nods and turns back to filling drinks, I head for the bathroom. The first thing I do is rip off my heels and stretch my toes. It feels so damn good, I moan. This job is definitely for the young, because I can't fathom still being here in ten years. After this year is done, I'll be moving on to bigger and better things.

I take my time freshening up, patting myself down with damp paper towels to cool my heated skin, and running my fingers through my hair. As I'm finishing up, the door to the women's restroom screams open, and I look up to see Bernice poke her head in.

"There you are," she says, sounding relieved. "I've been looking everywhere for you. Kota says you're needed in the VIP lounge." Her brown eyes flicker with amusement as her gaze drops to the foot I have planted in the sink basin.

It's the best relief I can get from those damn shoes, and I don't feel the least bit bashful about it. I lift my chin toward the paper towel dispenser, and Bernice rips a couple off, stretching her arm out to hand them to me.

"Did he say who it was?" Sometimes we get regulars. They're easy, because they're predictable.

But Bernice's scrunched nose tells me I won't like her answer. "Nope."

I sigh. After the day I've had, I'm not in the mood to entertain. "Well, do you know who it is?"

"Nope."

Great. This guy had better leave a big tip. "Let him know I'll be there in a minute."

"Will do, but a word to the wise, I wouldn't keep him waiting too long. The guy looks important." With a small smile, she ducks back out.

I sigh as I dry my feet and slip them back into the six-inch platforms. They pinch as I leave the bathroom, and I barely manage to paste on my happy face. I try to look on the bright side. I guess I'll get to put on a show after all.

***

The VIP room is located at the end of the single dark hall located off the main floor and to the right of the bar. It's lit by diffused neon pink lights and each of the six doors leading up to the last is closed, indicating that they're all in use. As I reach the end of the hall, I feel a flutter of nervous anticipation. I never know what I'm going to find once I open that door. One man, or two? Hot or not? There's no telling, but Bernice's words about him looking important give me a small ray of hope. Whatever the situation that I am about to walk into is, it's going to be more intimate than walking out onto that stage. And it's going to pay even better.

My hand shakes as I turn the handle and walk inside.

The room is larger than the rest, big enough for a party of twenty to fit into the bank of red leather booths forming a semi-circle along the far wall. Kota claims the leather gives customers the impression that the establishment is classy. In reality, anything looks classy when the only source of light comes from a fluorescent tube. It's just easier to clean up the mess when they're through. A circular stage with four gleaming silver metal poles sits in front of the booth and takes up the majority of the center of the room.

The wet bar to my right ensures that bachelors can get shitfaced while they have their dicks teased, but tonight, it stands empty.

This evening's venue is small, and as I set my eyes on the two figures seated directly across from me, I find myself wishing for a party.

A woman a few years older than me dressed in a black pencil skirt and plunging red blouse that matches her lipstick gives me an eager, heated look as I enter the room. She looks like a firecracker, and I decide to call her *Red*. Ten to one, this was her idea. Probably looking to spice things up in the bedroom. This often happens with couples coming for a dance together. It makes no difference to me. Money is money, and it's not my place to judge someone else's relationship. But I am judging, because I recognize the person beside her, the face staring back at me. I'd recognize that easy, laid back pose and those dark eyes anywhere.

Maybe it wasn't her idea, after all.

My worlds have collided again—merging like pools of mismatched paint spilled across the linoleum floor. I hadn't expected to see my mystery man again, but here he is, sitting in front of me, waiting for me to touch him. It's enough to steal my breath.

I don't know what he's doing here, and I hate that he brought someone with him, but I can't stop my eyes from eating up every inch of his delectable frame. He is a vision in a black suit, the first few buttons on his crisp white shirt undone to reveal a smattering of chest hair. As if that wasn't enough to convince me that he was up to no good, the crimson glow bathing him from above, makes him look like the devil—utterly sinful and impossible to deny.

Professor Scott's reluctance to reveal who he was meeting is no longer such a mystery. I wonder if he brought her here just to see how I'd react, maybe even as a punishment for attempting to dig for information. It's something I can see him doing. Whoever this woman is, she must be from out-of-town, because I certainly don't recognize her. I doubt very much that Professor Scott expected to run into his lover inside his classroom, just like I never expected for him to be one of my instructors. But my mystery man? Every move he makes is deliberate. Calculated. I have no doubt that tonight is a test of some kind.

I am out of my element. I feel betrayed, but at the same time, I remind myself there was never any commitment between us. Still, I can't shake the vision of him doing to her what he does to me in that hotel room.

Has she taken my place?

The thoughts racing through my head make me sick to my stomach. I'm a wobbling mess, and I need a fucking drink to calm my nerves, but to his credit, Professor Scott appears completely at ease. And why shouldn't he? He's the one pulling the strings here. It makes me wonder how often he does this. Although the knot that formed in my stomach the second I entered the door is becoming tighter and tighter with each step I take, he shows no signs of emotion. I can't tell if he's bothered by my presence, or if he's anticipating what's to come.

I'd like to think that's anticipation I'm reading in his eyes. Even though I never expected to give one of my professors a lap dance, I can't deny that a part of me is elated that I finally get the opportunity to get even closer to the man who has dominated my every thought and emotion for months. The more I think about it, the more I realize that I shouldn't even care that he has a girlfriend. He's entered *my* domain, and if anyone should be feeling uncomfortable right now, it's *him*. Tonight, I intend to show him what it feels like to be dominated.

Bolstered by this realization, I focus on the fact that I get to do to him what he has always done to me—sweet torture is my specialty. If he behaves, I might even let him touch me. The very idea of it makes me wet.

With slow, practiced movements, I set my knee on the stage and proceed to crawl across it. My eyes hold Professor Scott's as I twist around, seat myself on the edge, and plant my heels on either side of his and the woman's legs, spreading mine open wide. Professor's gaze drops to my crotch, and I smirk at the hunger I see in them.

It's the shot of courage I need.

"First rule: No talking." My voice cracks like a whip, bringing both their attention to my face. This isn't a house rule, but one of my own. I like my performances uninterrupted, and talking tends to ruin the mood. "If I ask you a question, a simple nod or shake of the head is all you need.

"Second rule: No touching. I will touch you, but you will not touch me...unless I let you," I add with a sultry smile as I meet Professor Scott's scorching gaze. He's no stranger to this rodeo. He knows the rules. But I have no doubt he'll break them in an instant if given an opening.

"Do we understand each other?" They both nod and my smile grows wider. "Excellent. Now, are we looking for a simple lap dance?"

The woman nods quickly, but her expression turns doubtful when she notices Professor sitting still as stone. My smile turns inward as I sense trouble on the horizon for this budding couple. I have no idea how long they've been together, but not knowing what each other wants is a sure sign of bad things to come. *I* know what he wants. *I* know exactly the kinds of dirty, nasty things get him off. Can she say the same?

"Since we're not on the same page, let's see if we can't get us there." I look at the woman, meeting her plain brown eyes. "For a basic dance, I'll start on the stage and work my way down to you two, clothes on at all times. If you're looking for more, clothes come off. Another step higher? I'll touch and fondle, get your man off, above or below the pants, and if I'm in the mood, I might let you touch me in return.

"Either or both of you can be involved. Some women like to watch me with their man." I look to Professor Scott. "Some men like to watch me with their woman. It's up to you two how you want to work it."

The heat I'd seen in Red's eyes when I first stepped into the room has been banked, and she now looks completely unsure of everything. I can almost read her mind. She's rethinking this whole night, wondering if she shouldn't have played it different. The idea of another woman grinding naked on her man isn't very appealing anymore.

I scoot back and pull myself up to stand on the stage. "I'll give you two a moment to think it over. Just don't take too long," I say as I grasp the pole and make a slow turn around it. "The clock is ticking."

I watch out of the corner of my eye as their heads meet and Red begins what appears to be a valiant effort to persuade Professor Scott to abandon this whole thing, but the way his gaze continuously slides up to look at me tells me he plans to stick around for the show.

Moments later, seeing Red throw herself back into the seat and cross her arms over her heaving chest, I have my answer. With a self-satisfied smile, I crouch down in front of them. "Are we decided?"

Professor Scott doesn't spare Red another glance. "I want the full experience."

Not *we*, but *I*. A small sense of victory grabs me, and I feel like purring. There is nothing sexier than a man who knows what he wants and isn't afraid to take it. It's why I've grown so fond of him. "You won't be disappointed."

I do as I outlined for them moments ago and work the pole, spinning, climbing, caressing until I'm certain that I have their full attention. The professor's dark eyes are dilated so much that they appear pure black, the pupil completely absorbed by the iris. As I ease off the stage and kneel in front of him, I see the large bulge running alongside his inner left thigh jump.

I'm trying to focus all of my attention on him and not on the irritated redhead watching us. It must be difficult to give up control to another woman, knowing that your boyfriend is getting off on her. But that's not my problem. Right now, he belongs to me.

Has always belonged to me.

The thought disturbs me, and I bury it before I can give it too much consideration. Blocking out any lingering nerves I have of finally being able to explore my fantasies of this man, I place my hands on his knees and skim them up his thighs, feeling the powerful muscles beneath twitch. Purposefully, I allow my fingertips to graze over that steel rod, and his sharp intake of breath fuels me.

When my breasts crush against his legs, I rub against him before crawling up the rest of his body, inhaling the rich combination of expensive cologne and brandy that clings to his tanned skin. Red grudgingly shifts over to make more space and avoid getting pierced by my heels, as I climb onto Professor Scott's lap to straddle him. Unable to resist, I run my fingers through his slicked back hair, then link them behind his neck. Throwing my head back, I rotate my hips to the beat of the music, my core brushing over his steel rod with each pass.

His low rumble of approval makes me wish we were somewhere else. Someplace where we could be alone and he was free to touch me, be inside of me. I've never found lap dances particularly appealing, but tonight, it's different. Tonight, it's the worst kind of tease. I've barely gotten started and my panties are soaked.

Lifting my head, I lock eyes with Professor Scott and lean forward, pressing my breasts against his face. I feel the wet drag of his tongue through my cleavage, igniting a maelstrom of desire inside me. Even though it's against the rules, I won't reprimand him. Instead, I reward him.

Sitting back, I continue to move seductively against him, maintaining eye contact as I run my hands over my breasts, squeezing them together, and then traveling higher to lift my hair off my neck. With deft fingers, I pull the bow to my top and let it fall, bearing my breasts to his hungry eyes. He's never allowed me to have this much control when we're together, and I intend to make the most of it.

Licking his lips, I see Professor's hands twitch at his sides, but like a good little boy, he doesn't touch me. Cupping my breasts again, I squeeze them together and pinch the nipples just as he would do, teasing them into hard points. The soft moans that fall past my lips don't have to be faked. I feel every tingle down to my core. If I didn't think Red would mind, I wouldn't stop at a lap dance.

The professor's cock is straining beneath me, and I can see from the dark look in his eyes that he's more than ready to explode. So am I.

Sitting up on my knees, I bring my breasts to his face, cupping them in offering, and drag the nipples across his lips. Seeing the question in his eyes, I bite my lip and nod my approval. We both want this, and without hesitation, Professor opens his mouth and latches onto my right breast. The feel of his hot, wet tongue on my breast nearly shatters me, and I pull free of his mouth with a loud smack. His glare is one of warning and disappointment. It excites me to no end.

Standing, I turn my back to him. Hooking my fingers in the thin fabric of my G-string, I slowly guide material down to my ankles. In this position, Professor doesn't have to guess how badly I want him. Even in the poor lighting, he'll be able to see my slick core weeping for him. And so will Red, who is growing more furious by the moment.

Kicking my wet panties aside, I sit down on his lap backward, and begin grinding my naked ass into his crotch. His cock is like a tree trunk between my cheeks, and holy shit, I can't help reliving what it felt like wedged inside of me this morning. No one save him has ever inspired this kind of reaction in me—this heightened awareness is threatening to kill me.

The slow rotation of my hips and pressure of my ass against his cock draws all kinds of deep, throaty sounds from the professor. I know, from this angle, he can see every inch of my naked form. The thought of allowing him to touch me in return is a temptation unlike anything I have ever experienced, but I refuse to give in to it. I want the professor to crave me like I crave him. I want him to leave tonight and think of me when he fucks his woman. I want to taint him for all others.

So, as I reach between my legs and tweak the sensitive bundle of nerves begging for attention, I work hard to bring us both to the edge of the proverbial cliff. And then, I jump.

Behind me, Professor Scott's breath hisses through his teeth and his chest pumps heavily against my back. Heat pours off him, and when he releases a painful groan and his body shudders, a smile grows on my face.

Standing, I bend and gather the pieces to my outfit. As I begin putting them back on, I turn around. My eyes are immediately drawn to the wet splotch visible through the dark material of the professor's perfectly pressed slacks.

"You'll find towels behind the bar if you'd like to clean yourself up before you leave, and Kota is out front if you'd like to schedule any future appointments. Just ask for Pussycat."

I leave before either of them can form a reply. Bernice is walking out of Room Three holding cleaning products in both hands, and I have to swerve to avoid running into her.

"Oh, hey, J," she calls out, trying to gain my attention, but I don't look back. Anything she has to say to me can wait. I continue walking toward the opposite end of the club and shut myself in the Employee's Only dressing room. My heart pounds inside my chest as the reality of what I have just done starts to sink in.

I just dry fucked my professor.

Six

Class the next morning is tense, to say the least. Although, I'm not sure whose side it's on more: mine or the professor's. I've kept my head and eyes down since the moment I walked into the room, unwilling to risk the knowing look I'll see in his eyes if I do.

I spent all night thinking about what happened in that darkened room and I know it was a mistake. I should have turned around and walked back out the second I laid eyes on him, but the temptation was too much. Now, I have to face what happened between us in the light of day, where secrets like ours become painfully transparent.

Despite how hard I have worked to keep the two sides of my world separate, they've collided in a way known for its total destruction. This isn't some J.Lo, *Maid in Manhattan* movie. It's a real life rush hour pile-up of epic proportions, and I can tell by the suffocating way the room closes in on me that it's going to require the Jaws of Life to get me out of this mess.

Even as I contemplate how I'm going to extract myself from this situation, I know my options are limited. This is the only Art Comp class on campus, and Professor Scott is the only professor in employ. Unless I want to change my major and completely derail all the plans I've spent the last four years working toward, then I have to suck it up and stay the course.

I've felt Professor Scott's eyes on me throughout the hour. My unwillingness to lift my eyes from my notebook and participate in the discussion may translate to my not paying attention. The reality of it couldn't be more opposite. I am painfully aware of every second that ticks by, of every deep-throated word that passes over his lips. I could recite every single thing he has said, I am that focused.

I also know right down to the second when the dismissal bell will ring. When it does, I'm out of my seat so fast, that Annie doesn't stand a chance of catching up. I can't help it. I need air. I need distance.

This pattern continues the rest of the week. It spills over into work. I find myself watching every shadowed corner, my insides a twisted mess, because I don't know whether I want to see that imposing figure lurking about or not.

But Professor Scott doesn't try to engage me in class, and he doesn't show up at the club. The week passes by without incident, and I begin to relax. No doubt, he feels just as off-kilter as I do. What happened between us is the kind of thing that causes scandals. It's what gets people fired from their job. For both our sakes, we need to forget that night—and every other night—ever happened.

I walk into DJ's, a bar located just off campus and search the crowded room. I'm supposed to meet Annie and a small group of our friends for drinks. I've been looking forward to it all week. The need to unwind and have some fun has stretched my nerves thin, and I feel about ready to snap. After the week I've had, this couldn't have come at a better time.

Spotting our group at a table close to the stage where a local band is playing a cover of Weezer's *Back to the Shack*, I wend my way through the crowd. My smile stretches ear-to-ear when I spot Annie sitting at the head of the table, her cheeks already flushed from the beer she holds in her left hand.

Approaching from the side, I hook her around the neck and pull her in for a hug before she can register it's me. Her screech of surprise is short-lived, and then she is popping out of her chair to embrace me. "You made it!"

"You're drunk!" I hold her away from me, laughing as I take in her glassy eyes and flushed cheeks.

Annie wags her finger at me as we both sit down at the table. "Tipsy, not drunk. You can't get drunk off one beer."

I raise my brows. "If you say so, doll. So, where's your boy toy?" I glance around the table, seeing no sign of Jason.

"He's going to be late." She rolls her eyes. I can see why the party started without me.

Patting her hand in understanding, I open my mouth to offer some form of comfort, but am yanked out of my chair and into a strong pair of arms before I can utter a word.

"You come in and can't even say hi?"

I laugh as the breath is squeezed out of me. "Brody! I didn't see you when I came in." I give him a peck on his whiskered cheek. "Even if I had, you know I have to show my girl some love before anyone else."

Standing more than six inches taller than me, I have to look up into Brody's smiling brown eyes as he sets me back on my feet. His wide, white smile and deep dimples are catnip to the average female population, and even I have to admit that I am not immune to his charms. But

I've known Brody since he was a scrawny freshman, and have come to see him as a brother.

"I've known you longer," he pouts.

"Sisters before misters," I say, playfully punching him in his rock solid arm. Thanks to football, the man is built. Just another reason he's such a lady-killer.

"And bros before hoes. You hanging out a while? Rio's signed up for Karaoke and is hoping you'll join him."

"Oh no!" I hold up my hands and shake my head. "I'm off duty tonight."

"What? You have to go. You make the perfect June."

I made the mistake of singing "Walk the Line" once with Rio while drunk off my ass, and have allowed myself to be roped into singing it every weekend since. Tonight, I'm throwing in the towel.

Laughing, I back away toward the bar with my hands in the air. "Sorry, but Johnny's going to have to go solo tonight. Unless you want to lend him a hand?" Flashing him a crude gesture, I spin around and disappear into the crowd.

If possible, it's more crowded at the bar. And loud, too. I have to shout over the blaring music to get the bartender's attention, and even then, I get nowhere. Turns out, my voice is too mousy to carry over the swell of noise.

I'm leaning over the counter, waving my hand to gain the older man's attention, when I feel a wall of heat press against my side. Turning my head, I look over my shoulder and feel time screech to a sudden halt.

Professor Scott looks down at me, his dark eyes like lasers that sear right through me. My breathing falters and I ease back until my toes touch the solid floor. A breath of air is the only thing standing between us. Tonight, he's swapped out his more subdued teaching attire for the sexy, dark, tailored look. The black pants make him appear long and lean, but I find my eyes drawn to the powder pink button-down, two buttons open to reveal a hint of chest hair. The sight takes me back to the VIP room, and a rush of heat burns through my entire body.

I recall his dark eyes filled with a combination of warning and lust. It's the same look he's giving me now, only ten times more intense. This is the kind of man who dominates in his relationships. He screams danger, but it's not the kind I want to run away from. Rather, it's the kind that draws a person in, lulls them into a false sense of security, and after taking them places they've never imagined, tears them apart and leaves them lying in tatters.

Still, like a helpless moth, I can't help wanting to get closer. I'm drawn to his heat. I want to be burned.

He is the devil on my shoulder.

Even knowing this, I can't turn away.

"You look like you could use a drink." His voice is deeper than usual, and I wonder if that's because he's as affected by me as I am by him. Lifting his arm, I study his strong profile while he orders our drinks. I don't realize how hard I'm staring until he holds up a glass in front of my face, a knowing smirk tugging at his full lips.

"Shit, thanks." I down the amber liquid, gasping as it burns a path down my throat.

"That was mine, actually." I blink rapidly, trying to focus through the sting and make sense of his words. He holds up a beer. "This would be yours."

My cheeks flame and I burst out laughing, shaking my head as I take the bottle. "Oops. Sorry about that. I'll buy you another."

Instead of arguing, he lets me, watching in amusement as I attempt to flag down the bartender. It takes several tries before I finally give up and motion to him. With impressive skill, he uses his commanding voice to bring the guy over. I wish I had one of those—a booming voice, that is. Not only is it sexy as hell, but it can't be ignored. At least, not the way Professor Scott uses it. Once again, I am transported back to that hotel room, to the way he commands my body and mind so effortlessly.

After he is served a fresh brandy, he watches me over his glass as he takes a taste. "So, you come here often?" he asks with a hint of amusement.

"Every Saturday."

His brows lift in question. "No work on Saturdays?"

He's baiting me, and I refuse to bite. "Nope. Saturdays are my *play* days." I emphasize "play" hoping to garner some kind of reaction, but I get none. Saturday is the only day I requested off when I started working at the club, for obvious reasons. It's the true start of the weekend, the one day I get to let down my hair and forget about work and school and immerse myself in pleasure, and I use it to my full advantage.

He hums and nods thoughtfully. "Here with friends?"

Peering over his head, I lift my chin, indicating Annie and the group that is now gathered around her, smiling and laughing, and all without me. "Looks like the gang is all here."

Professor Scott glances over his shoulder, but his interest is not with them. When his eyes meet mine again, the hunger is plain for anyone to see, and a thread of anticipation tangles in my belly. "I've never been to this establishment. Stick around and have a drink with me."

The low rumble of his voice does things to me, but as tempting as the offer is, I made myself a promise, and I need to stick to it. "Sorry, no. That's probably not the best idea, wouldn't you agree? I should be getting back." Taking my beer with me, I step away from the bar.

Catching my hand in his, he holds me in place. I wait for him to say something—anything—until I realize that it isn't what I'm waiting for him to say that I should be paying attention to—it's what he's *not* saying.

It's all right there, in the knowing, teasing gleam in those onyx eyes. Lust. Intrigue. *Promise.* This isn't over between us. Not by a long shot.

I can still feel the imprint of his fingers on my skin, long after I make my escape.

Seven

I lost count of how many drinks I had around number seven. Seeing as seven is my lucky number, I can't go wrong. Stepping onto that stage tonight seems like a pretty good idea from where I'm standing, which is on top of my chair.

"If you don't stop shaking your ass like that," Brody chides, "you're gonna bust an ankle."

I glance down at my heeled blue suede boots and shake my head. It spins in response, which sends all of my senses into a tailspin. I throw my hands out to steady the walls, feeling like I might throw up. "These shoes would never hurt me," I slur, knowing I'm right because Elvis would never steer me wrong.

Shaking his head, Brody returns his attention to the stage where a female duo is wrapping up their version of *Wind Beneath My Wings*.

It's at that moment that the chair slides out from under me.

I screech as I begin falling, but before anyone at the table has time to react, a pair of strong arms catch me just in the nick of time. I'm so happy I didn't break my ass that I cling to my savior like a bur.

Until I realize who is holding me.

Black-as-midnight eyes glare back at me, as though I've done something to personally offend him, and I shove out of Professor Scott's arms, rolling awkwardly to my feet. He's such a gentleman, though, that he refuses to relinquish his hold on my arm until he's certain I won't make a repeat performance.

"What are you still doing here?" I brush any dirt I may have picked up from my clothes.

"I think the question is what are *you* still doing here? How many drinks have you had tonight? Because I counted seven."

Well, what's the point in asking if he's just going to answer for me? I lift my chin a little higher. "I know my limit."

He leans closer, placing his lips against my ear. "Yeah? Then why are you swaying on your feet right now?" As if to prove his point, the room tilts and I pitch sideways. Grasping my arms, Professor Scott holds me upright. Which is good, because I am pretty sure my legs have turned to rubber.

Maybe he has a point.

"Come on, you've had enough for tonight. I'll drive you home."

"I'm not ready to go home yet. I have a performance and I can't miss it."

"The only performance in your future is climbing into bed and sleeping it off." Focusing on something over my head, Professor Scott says, "We're heading out."

Baffled, I turn to see who he is speaking to and see Brody nod in agreement. "Cool. I'll have someone follow me over in the morning to drop off her car."

"Wait, you two know each other?" I ask, fighting through the alcohol-induced fog.

"Who, Ransom?" Brody asks as he abandons his chair to join us at the end of the table. "He's the art teacher." He says this as if everyone knows this, which maybe they do. The man is gorgeous. You'd have to be dead not to notice him.

Ransom. So that's his name. It's... hot. Dangerous, just like I know him to be. I wonder just how much *Ransom* has told Brody about us. But the fact that Brody isn't beating his face in right now suggests not a lot.

"He's gonna take you home, okay, kid?" Brody's massive hand lands on top of my head and gives it a little shake. Hair falls in my eyes, and I shake him free in annoyance. "I'm gonna need your keys before you go."

"My keys? What if I say no?"

Brody gives me his trademark crooked smile that says he finds me funny. "You're wasted, and I already made the arrangements. Do me a favor and cooperate for once. I'll make sure your car is waiting for you when you wake up tomorrow."

I'm not sure how I feel about him going behind my back, but the alcohol is starting to get to me and I don't think to question it further. My chest constricts at how nice Brody is to me. He's such a good guy. It literally brings a tear to my eye. I sniff and wipe it away as I hand over the keys. "Don't hurt her."

"Not unless she asks me to." Smirking, Brody pulls me into a quick hug and then hands me back to Ransom. "I don't care if she asks you to, don't hurt her. Got it?"

"You have my word."

***

I don't live far, and Ransom has no problem following my directions. Surprising considering I can't quite remember how to get home right now. With a hand on my arm to help steady me, he walks me to my door and uses my keys to let me inside.

"Thanks for seeing me home safely," I say as I step inside and feel around for the light switch.

"Do you need any help with anything before I go?"

Looking back at him, the slight frown Ransom wears confuses me. I'm not sure if he was hoping I'd tell him no so he can leave, or if he wants me to ask him inside. "I'll be fine," I assure him. It's probably best that he leave anyway. There is nothing cute about being drunk, and I am pretty sure I'm going to be worshiping the porcelain god soon.

Bending to take off my shoes, I have a difficult time maintaining my balance. Using the wall for support, I succeed, though barely. The sound of the door closing behind me is startling, and my head jerks up. "I thought you left."

Ransom shakes his head. "You can barely stand. I'd be angry at myself if I didn't at least stick around long enough to make sure you made it to your bed."

I don't know how I feel about him being in my personal, private space. With a relationship like ours, this kind of thing isn't supposed to happen. He isn't supposed to know my name, who I spend my time with, or where I live. In a week's time, that careful balance has been shattered.

The kindness in his dark eyes is surprising, though. There's something different about him tonight, but I can't quite put my finger on it. The

J . C . V a l e n t i n e | **65**

man I know never had a look that I would call
"kind." *Predatory* is more like it. Is this the man
he really is outside the bedroom? Not that I am
complaining. What girl doesn't like being taken
care of?

Placing a hand on my lower back, he urges
me on. "Come on, let's get you tucked in."

Following my lead, we walk together
through the hallway that connects my minute
living and dining rooms with the even smaller
kitchen, bathroom, and single bedroom. It is such
a tiny space that it only takes a few steps before
we are standing outside the door. Staring at my
queen-sized bed, I can't decide what my next
move will be.

On the one hand, I really want sleep. On
the other, I really need the bathroom. As drained
as I am, I know I have to take care of one before I
can do the other. "I need to…" I point to the
bathroom behind us, my cheeks feeling flushed.

Taking a step back, Ransom gives me
enough space to get by. "While you do that, I'll
go get you a glass of water."

I nod, thankful that he is giving me
distance, and close the door. After spending a
solid five minutes hanging over the toilet bowl
and realizing that I haven't quite reached the point
of no return, I relieve myself and take a minute to
scrub my face clean of makeup and pull my hair
back. When I run out of things to do, I return to

the bedroom to find Ransom sitting on the edge of the mattress.

The sight of him there makes my blood simmer. Screw personal space. I like the idea of having him in my bed, of his rich cologne permeating my sheets.

He stands as I walk in. "I found a bucket under the sink, in case you need it later. Water is on the table. Do you need me to bring you anything from the bathroom, aspirin or Tylenol?"

How incredibly...sweet. I study his offerings, unable to keep the smile off my face. "This is perfect," I tell him. I'm used to taking care of myself, so this is a treat. "That was very thoughtful of you. Thank you."

His eyes widen a fraction and I step closer. Placing my hands on his chest, I reach up on my toes to show him my gratitude. My lips graze his, and the fleeting contact is electric.

"What are you doing, Josephine?" Grasping my wrists, he draws his head back and forces me away from him. The stern look in his eyes is confusing. He's denying me?

"I was thanking you." I try to step into him again, but his firm hold ensures I keep my distance.

"You're drunk," he says, dismissing me entirely. What. The. Hell.

"Ransom, I'm not *that* drunk," I protest.

"Well, then, I'm going to pretend that you are." Dropping my wrists, Ransom turns his back on me and begins walking away.

"Ransom! Wait, don't go!" Even though the voice inside my head suggests that I leave well enough alone, that this is the way it's supposed to be, I can't keep myself from running after him.

Once he reaches the front door, Ransom rounds on me. "What did you think was going to happen here tonight, Miss Hart?"

My jaw drops at the formality, and I flounder for words. "I—I don't know. You'd stay the night maybe?"

His head drops to his chest and he shakes it in disbelief. "I'm your teacher. You're my student."

He was really going to pull this card on me? I understand the confusion. I feel it, too. But there is no sense in pretending that nothing has happened between us. He had his mouth on my nipples just days ago, and I know the taste of his cock well. Pretending none of it ever happened doesn't mean it will just go away. I know. I tried. And look where it's gotten me.

"Then why bring me home? Why come inside?" I challenge.

Scraping his hands through his hair, he lifts his gaze and I can see the war being waged inside him. "You're a nice girl, Josephine. I knew you'd had too much to drink tonight, and when your friend asked me to do him a favor and take you home, I said yes. I was just trying to help."

Sure he was. Or maybe he got closer than he intended and is running away. Where has my confident, take-charge mystery man gone? I much prefer him over the one standing in front of me. If only I could turn back the clock and choose a different path.

Instead of being the complacent little mouse I have always been for him, I get angry. "Thanks for all your help, but I've got it from here." Crossing my arms, I glare at him. I just want him out of my apartment. I haven't completely forgiven him for bringing that woman to me, and I am furious that he would come all this way just to walk out. I feel like a fool, running after him when he clearly doesn't want to be chased.

Well, I'm done.

Sighing, Ransom opens the door. His hand freezes on the knob as he looks back at me. "I'm sorry I upset you. You're an attractive girl, and you seem really nice, but I just can't go there. When you wake up in the morning, you'll see that, too."

Although his words ring true, I don't care to hear them.

"And Miss Hart?" Regret shines in his dark eyes. "From now on, I think it would be best if we stick to formalities."

For some reason, that really stings, almost as much as knowing he's slept with another woman. As he closes the door behind him, I scoop up one of my black pumps and lob it at the door. Then I flip the lock so he can't come back.

From here on out, Ransom Scott is dead to me.

Eight

My outlook is good come Monday morning. After spending the remainder of the weekend catching up on homework and wallowing in self-pity, I am resolved to start fresh. Nothing of the past week will affect my time moving forward, and anytime my thoughts attempt to stray toward the past, I shove it into a little black box in the back of my mind.

That plan goes to shit the moment I enter the classroom and see Ransom sitting at his desk. He's dressed casually in tan slacks, a light blue button-down shirt with a navy sweater-vest overtop. His head is bent over, one hand delved deep into his tousled black hair, the other writing something in red pen.

Annie is absent today, and I want to kill her for leaving me to my fate, but I'm also grateful, because it allows me to escape. With hurried strides, I bypass my usual seat in the front row and claim one at the back of the room.

I try my best to remain invisible throughout the next hour. I slump in my seat, keep my head down, and volunteer for nothing. When Ransom hands down our final assignment for the semester, I groan inwardly. We have to find a way to *inspire* art. I don't know what that means exactly, but he assured us that as the class progresses, it will become clearer. Of course, if we have any questions, he is always available after class.

I'd rather Google it.

The bad thing about being in the back of the room is that it prevents an easy escape. I do my best to blend in with my classmates, and as the door draws nearer, I think I have succeeded, until I hear my name.

"Miss Hart, can I see you for a moment?"

Those nine words chill me to the bone. My head droops on my shoulders. *Why me?* Taking a deep breath, I turn and make my way back into the room, stopping several feet from Ransom's desk.

He is busily tucking papers into his leather briefcase when I approach and it takes a moment for him to acknowledge me. "I noticed you hiding in the back today. Any particular reason for that?"

"I prefer the back of the room."

He nods, seeming to understand. "Does this have anything to do with Saturday night?"

My arms clench tighter around my books. "I'm afraid I had a few too many drinks with my friends Saturday night. My memory is a little foggy." A lie, but when cornered like prey, sometimes it's the only chance of escape.

Snapping the case closed, Ransom lays it flat on the desk, and then presses his palms into the soft material. "I understand if you feel uncomfortable around me, but I want you to know that I have zero interest in complicating matters any further than they already are. My job is on the line, so if it's okay with you, I'd like to put this weekend behind us and move forward."

"As if nothing happened?" My lip curls at the idea. It's what I wanted, but hearing those words come from his mouth somehow makes them more real. His willingness to walk away from me makes my stomach lurch.

Those midnight orbs lift, and I swear I see the same pain and confliction in them that I feel inside of me. Could it be that he doesn't want this any more than I do? That he, too, longs for our time together. "*Nothing* happened, and that's the way it needs to stay."

I hear the growl in his voice and even though I know it's wrong, my body responds. I feel the flames of desire licking between my legs, making my nipples grow tight. *Does he have any idea what he does to me?*

I'm not sure how to take his words. Is he just saying that because it's the right thing, the only way to cover his ass, or is it because he really believes that what we have shared together amounts to nothing?

Both possibilities are difficult to face, because there can be no good outcome either way, but I still want it, even if he doesn't. "So where does this leave us?" I ask, using my books as a shield against my feelings for him. Ransom is the only man who has ever affected me this way—he can strip me bare with a single look. He can reduce me from a strong, intelligent, educated woman into a puddle of wanton desire with the stroke of a finger.

Pushing his hands into his pockets as he comes to stand before me, I realize, with a mix of horror and intrigue, that this man is the only one that has ever held the power to hurt me.

He holds my gaze as he stares down at me, and I see the muscle in his jaw tick in time with my heartbeat. We're connected in a way that neither of us fully realizes, and I feel the draw to him growing stronger. "This leaves us right where we stand, with me as your professor and you as my student."

The deep rasp of his voice triggers something deep inside of me, and I feel myself lean closer. The allure of those full lips is nearly impossible to deny. You can tell so much from a simple kiss. I want his on me—on the most intimate parts of my body—and I want him to know that.

His gaze drops to my mouth, and even though I know I shouldn't, I need to kiss him. If this is it between us, then I need this last connection, this final goodbye.

"Miss Hart." My name is a low warning as it whispers past his lips, but I ignore it.

"Please, call me Josephine," I whisper just before my mouth closes over his. I don't know who moans first. If Ransom meant for us to go our separate ways, then I probably shouldn't have kissed him, because the way he is kissing me back definitely isn't a goodbye.

His mouth is hesitant at first, as if he is unsure what to do. I understand his confliction. This is the worst case scenario, a student falling for her professor. Movies have been made about this sort of thing, but neither of us heeds the warning.

It doesn't take long for him to throw himself into the deep end, though, and then we're both drowning, surrendering to the torrent of emotion rushing between us. I've never felt a man surrender, much less this man, who is normally so aggressive, but he is definitely giving in to me now.

I am still clutching my books to my breasts, which have grown swollen and heavy, and his hands are still shoved deeply into his pockets. The only part of us that is touching is our mouths, but Ransom's wet tongue probing the inside of my mouth is like a full body caress. It takes me back to our hotel room, and I start imagining what it would be like to have him bend me over his desk, pull down my pants, and take me right now.

That fantasy is shattered when I hear voices approaching. I break the kiss first. Ransom stares at me with some emotion I can't name. His breathing is labored, his lids heavy, eyes dilated, and the bulge in his pants is unmistakable. He looks like how I feel—hot, raw, and aching, the need to touch and be touched almost too powerful to ignore.

But I can ignore it, because we're no longer alone, and I won't risk him losing his job. I would never do anything to hurt him, just as I instinctively know he would never do anything to hurt me. For as complicated as our relationship may be, we have a mutual respect for each other that runs deep. We give each other pleasure, and in return, we respect and protect each other's privacy.

"You should go," he says, his voice a guttural rasp so thick, he has to clear his throat.

I love that I can affect him this way. It gives me a rare sense of power that I typically only experience on-stage. "See you tomorrow, Mr. Scott." I back away, smiling. The last image I have of him is his dark scowl, but it doesn't concern me, because as much as Professor Ransom Scott might say we're done, I know the truth.

We're just getting started.

***

Work Wednesday night is a bitch. The first thing I hear upon entering *Mirage* is, "Tamera called in sick. You're headlining tonight."

My head whips up in shock, seeing Kota standing there in his open leather vest, showing off a toned physique and a dusting of dark, curly hair. His expression is grim but expectant.

"Headlining?" Thrown by his announcement, my hands pause in the task of latching my bra. That spot is reserved for the most popular dancer. It took Tamera years to work up to that position. "Why not one of the other girls? Someone who's been here longer?"

"Because no one holds a candle to you, Pussycat," he says with a smirk. "You're on in ten."

I'm left standing alone in the middle of the dressing room in nothing but a bra and thong, my mouth gaping open. As the seconds tick by, a slow smile creeps into place. Headlining is the highest form of praise here. I could make rent with the tips from one dance alone. It is in that moment I like to think my parents are looking down at me from above, giving me that little boost I so desperately needed.

With tears in my eyes, I whisper, "Thank you," then I suit up for the hottest performance of my life.

Nine

I take a double shot of whiskey as I stand offstage waiting to be announced. As happy as I am to have this opportunity fall into my lap, I would be lying if I said I wasn't a nervous wreck. In the span of ten minutes, I have considered twenty different ways to back out. I can't shake the thought that this isn't my show. I'm not supposed to be up there. I haven't earned this.

To be honest, despite the financial benefits, I'm not sure I want this.

Being a headliner means standing under a different kind of spotlight. Even though most of these men are regulars, I don't know how keen I am with the idea of being their central focus. And I will be if I go through with this.

This was never Plan A or B. Stripping was a mean to an end. Going up on that stage tonight could change everything, but I'd be stupid to pass this up. I just want to make my money and leave. That's been my goal since day one, and it's my goal tonight.

As Felicia's song ends and she steps offstage, I pull at the hem of my shirt and straighten the tie hanging between my breasts. Tonight, I'm going farther than I ever have before. The idea that Ransom could be out there watching makes every cell in my body ignite. But it's only Wednesday.

My feet teeter in my heels as I step up the single stair onto the stage and stand just beyond the curtains, out of sight.

The room is plunged into darkness, as per my usual request. It gives me the time I need to walk onto the stage unnoticed, and take my place. Stretching my arm up, I let my head fall back and close my eyes.

Blue lights begin to spin around the room, fog crawls across the stage, and I hear Kota's growl over the sound system as he announces me. There are no cheers, no clapping hands, just the music as it filters down from the ceiling and expands throughout the building. Then the spotlight hits me, and I begin to move.

"Hot for Teacher" is my song of choice, kind of a personal joke. I know Ransom isn't here to hear it, but if he was, I imagine he'd be laughing right along with me. As I grind my hips and do my turns around the pole, I find myself hoping that he is here. I lack the guts to look. Even though I am used to the job, I will never get used to the exposure of it. Power or not, the idea of performing in front of a crowd is unnerving. The only way to survive the anxiety that threatens to creep up on me is to ignore everything and just dance.

The music consumes me, and I remind myself that this is a special performance. In order to be the head dog, I have to perform like one. Channeling my inner vixen, the one that gyrated in her lover-slash-professor's lap while his girlfriend watched, I drag my palms over my hips and up my sides, following the swell of my breasts as they continue to climb higher. Lifting my long hair, I release my top and let it flutter to the stage.

Every woman has a favorite part of their body. Mine are my breasts. They're round and full with smooth, pale skin and pert pink nipples. Any man I've ever been with has had nothing but nice things to say about them, so I am confident in showing them off now.

It's as I stand, whipping my hair back from my face, that I feel the intensity of *His* stare. I can't see past the gloom I've set for myself, but I know he's here. My insides turn molten instantly as I drop to my knees and thrust my hips. I'm on fire, thinking of our earlier kiss, of the way his hands feel on my skin, the scorching heat of his body against mine.

I can't think straight, and when the music ends, I miss my cue. The lights rise before I do, and I feel the horror of seeing dozens of eyes plastered to my naked body, but then my gaze lands on one set in particular and a curious sense of calm comes over me.

Ransom's smirk is contagious, and as he leaves his table and makes his way toward me, anticipation pours over me like hot candle wax— breathtaking, scalding, thrilling.

Standing, I collect my top and exit stage left.

I'm not in the dressing room for more than thirty seconds when the door opens and Bernice pokes her head inside. "Joe, that man from the other night is here to see you. He says you know each other?" She looks uncertain, but I wave my hand.

"Let him in." Running a brush through my hair, I watch in the mirror as Ransom walks up behind me. Even in the low light, his dark eyes and hair are striking against his sun-kissed skin, and as he moves closer, his arrogant gaze travels down my body. Settling his strong hands firmly on my hips, he dips his head to trace his nose along the side of my neck.

"Damn, you smell delicious."

The stubble on his cheek scrapes over my skin, causing every nerve ending in my body to tingle. It's like pins and needles, only it feels good. "Ra—uh, Mr. Scott," I quickly correct myself, reminded of his preference for formalities. "I thought you were done with this?"

I watch his expression for something, anything, but it remains fully focused as he continues to explore my nakedness with hands and mouth. Everywhere he makes contact feels like a burn. "Done with what?"

"With us," I say, an embarrassing moan leaving me as his hand boldly sneaks beneath my thong and traces through my wetness.

"I could never be done with this," he groans, his voice pitching lower before sinking his teeth into my shoulder. "Fuck, you're so damn wet. I was going to order us dinner before I took you to bed, but your sweet pussy just ruined all of that."

His fingers push through my slick folds and plunge inside, tearing a moan from me. Distantly, I hear the clink of his belt buckle, followed by the lowering of his zipper. I gasp at the sudden emptiness as he pulls his fingers out of me, and then I hear as much as feel my thong torn from my waist. I'll feel that later, but for now, the only pain I want to pay attention to his hard cock pounding into me.

"Bend that sweet ass over," he commands as he wraps his hand around my nape and shoves me down, forcing me to throw out my hands and brace myself against the vanity. Grabbing his cock, I watch him in the mirror as he rubs it between my legs.

"You're a tease," he accuses as he slaps his cockhead against my aching clit. "You made me come in my pants."

Breathless, I say, "I didn't hear you complaining."

His hand lands hard on my ass, and I scream from the sting of it. My arousal turns painful. "My date didn't like it."

"Oh?" I pant, reeling from the word *date*. Not girlfriend. Date. The bastard. But I don't feel sorry for what I did. Instead, I feel anger take root in my gut, and I'm unable to keep the bite from my words. "Didn't she enjoy watching you clean away the mess I made?"

"No," he says wickedly, meeting my gaze in the mirror. "She especially didn't enjoy having to lap it up with her tongue."

I want to laugh even as jealousy tears through me. He let another woman touch him, taste him. Not that it was a big surprise, but suspecting and knowing are two different things.

"Too bad *she* couldn't make you come in your pants. Maybe she'd be the one riding your dick tonight instead."

"Who says she didn't?"

My eyes narrow, and I am ready to tell him to fuck off, when he shoves his cock into my ass. His hand clamps over my mouth before my scream has a chance to carry. Moisture burns my eyes as he pounds into me. I've never grown used to his size and being untried *there*, verges on excruciating.

Stars float behind my closed eyelids as I struggle to even out my breathing. Ransom continues to take me hard, making it difficult, if not impossible, to do. I'd tell him no, but he loves it, and I love pleasing him. Even if it means I won't be able to sit down right later.

I'm a sick person, I know this. Ransom doesn't deserve me, and I deserve so much better than him. Trouble is, I can't seem to make myself walk away. One look, one touch, that's all it takes, and I'm back under his spell.

"I love fucking your tight little hole," he growls into my ear, and presses in deeper, holding his hips against mine long enough for me to feel the full length of him. "You think it was funny messing up my pants? I wonder if you'll be laughing when I fill your pretty little ass with my cum."

I'm sure I won't be laughing at all. His filthy words stir something inside of me, and despite the weakness in my knees, feel an orgasm lurking in the shadows. I won't give the thought voice, but I want him to fill me. I love feeling his juices leak down my thighs after he uses me, hard. It's his mark, his own personal brand, and I wear it proudly.

If he knew the way I really felt, turned on by his aggressive, deviant behavior, he'd drop me faster than I can blink. He doesn't have to tell me this for me to know it's true. Ransom is the kind of man who gets off on instilling a little bit of fear. I can see it in his eyes, which is why I will never let on how much I love it.

A few squeaks of surprise, a couple of moans, and some heavy panting are all it takes to push him over the edge. I don't get mine, but he pumps his hot semen into my ass with a roar so loud I'm afraid someone will barge in to investigate.

Still lodged deep inside me, Ransom's softer side makes an appearance as he pulls me up and wraps his arm around me, holding my back to his chest, ensuring I don't fall over. It's a big possibility, considering how wobbly my legs feel right now. He lingers long enough that his cock shrinks back, slipping from my body of its own accord. Semen wets my cheeks and inner thighs, slowly leaking back out as I stand up straight. Turning me in his arms, Ransom smoothes my hair back from my face and flashes me a lazy but devastating smile.

"I'm staying in room two-oh-five. I'll have dinner waiting when you get there." Gripping my chin, he tilts my head back and his mouth covers mine, his tongue sliding over my lips and into my mouth before he releases me. After tucking himself back into his pants, he reaches into his wallet and hands me a key card. "Let yourself in."

I bite my lip as I watch him turn to leave. This man confuses me. One minute he's a brute, laying waste to my body and emotions, and the next, he's almost sweet. I wish I could figure him out, but he's like a puzzle that's impossible to solve.

Studying the hard piece of plastic in my hand, I find myself questioning the wisdom of meeting him tonight. I know I'm waffling, set on walking away one minute, and diving back into bed with him the next, but I don't know how to turn my back on this man. Not certain I even want to. The only thing I know for certain is how I feel when he's standing in front of me—*alive*. I've never felt more alive than in the moments we steal.

Ransom is my drug. Each time I feast on his body, I fall deeper into my addiction. Tonight, even with my ass already beginning to ache, I know I will show up at his door. The secrecy shrouding our relationship should cause me shame. I know he's hiding something from me. I used to think he was just a businessman who breezed into town a few nights a month to fuck me senseless and leave again, but now I know different. So what reason would a man who lives in the same city I do have to rent a hotel room, unless he has a secret?

The fact is, even though a part of me cares, it's not enough. My desire for him is more powerful than his truth. Without another thought, I clean myself up and get dressed.

Ten

"You didn't have to do this." Annie steps back to allow me inside her apartment.

When she texted me early this morning telling me not to wait for her before class, I panicked. The idea of going in alone gave me hives. So I did the only thing I could think of—ransacked the kitchen cabinets for a can of Campbell's Chicken Noodle and showed up on her doorstep an hour later, fully prepared to play nursemaid.

"You're sick. I bring soup." Heading straight for the kitchen, I pour the chicken noodle soup from the container into a soup cup made by the same company, nuke it in the microwave, and return to the living room where I find her curled up in a corner of the couch. "You look like death warmed over," I say as I hand her the bowl.

She looks at it with a mix of longing and repulsion, and then takes a tiny sip. "Campbell's, Joe? You shouldn't have." The mirth in her eyes gives me a chuckle.

"It's double noodle, too," I point out as I take a careful seat across from her. After spending the night with Ransom, it's a miracle I can even walk. I count my blessings, because that man is unequaled when it comes to his skills in the sack.

After taking a couple more bites, she sighs, sets the bowl on the table, and curls back under the blanket draped around her shoulders.

"So, what's going on with you? Flu? Bad breakup?" I ask hopefully. I haven't forgotten about Jason's inability to show up at the bar last week, and I am holding firm to my conviction that she needs to drop him on his ass, and fast.

Annie rolls her eyes. "You wish."

"I really do."

"It's complicated," she says softly, then burrows deeper into her blanket.

"What's complicated about saying 'Hey, we should see other people'? The guy is a douche. Do you have any idea how many guys at school would kill to go on a date with you?"

I'm not even exaggerating. Annie is the kind of girl that sparks men's primal instincts. She's got that whole cute and innocent vibe about her. Hell, most days, even I want to wrap my arms around her and shelter her from the world.

"It just is, Joe, and I don't really want to talk about it right now. What's up with you?" she asks, changing the subject. I let her, only because I don't want to fight when she clearly needs her rest. "Don't think I didn't notice you limping in here."

Shit. I thought I had done a pretty decent job of masking the Quasimodo routine. That's what I get for letting Ransom use me so hard last night. My only solace comes from knowing that I used him just as hard. With any luck, he's feeling it too this morning. I scoff, waving her comment off. "I was not limping. I just strained a muscle is all."

"Mmm hmm. Let me guess, yoga really kicked your ass this morning?"

Not yoga, I think to myself. I can tell by her amused expression that she isn't buying my excuse. She's always been able to see right through me, so I don't even know why I bother trying to lie.

I feel a sudden wave of doubt slam into me. She doesn't have it together any more than I do, but I still consider asking her for advice. It's selfish of me, and yet, maybe it will make her feel better to focus on something other than her screwed up love life.

"Annie..." I hesitate. How to form this question? "Assume you know someone who is involved with someone that they probably shouldn't be."

Perking up, I now have her full attention. "Is this someone I know?"

"Purely hypothetical."

She purses her lips. "Okay, I have no idea who these fictional people are, but they're in a relationship?"

"It's more sex than a relationship," I clarify. "But what if one of them wants it to be more than that?"

"I guess it depends on who the other person is and what they want. What are they like?"

"Well, they're both smart, serious about their career, friendly, and attractive. They have a lot in common, actually."

"That's a start. What are they like *together*?"

I look toward the window framing the back of the couch and choose my words carefully. "They have fun. Sometimes they laugh, but mostly it's very intense. Recently they've been spending some time together outside of their normal routine, and it's making things…complicated."

Annie frowns as she studies me. I shift uncomfortably under her close scrutiny, fearing she'll be able to see right through me. "If these two people have agreed to have a purely sexual relationship, and one of them is changing their mind, then I think that person has a duty to tell the other person how they're feeling so they can decide how to proceed."

"What if the other person decides they want to end the relationship?"

"It's a risk, but in the end, it would protect both of them. Staying too long in a relationship that isn't working anymore can do more damage than good."

I raise a brow at her remark and she purses her lips again, receiving the silent message. "Well, what if one of them is getting mixed signals," I press on. "For example, what if they can't tell what the other person is feeling because each time they see the other person, they're different."

Annie is quiet for a long time as she mulls this over. I wait patiently, because it's either sit here and do nothing or go to class and face Ransom. When I left his room this morning, he was the same distant and dismissive man he was last week. If I attend his class only to have him look at me with softness and caring again, I'm going to scream. Hiding out in this apartment for a few hours seems like the safest bet at the moment.

"I think if this person has to think so hard about their relationship status, then maybe it's not worth the trouble," Annie finally says. "Relationships are supposed to make you feel good. Whether it's love or purely sex, there shouldn't be any question about who feels what for whom or what's going to happen next, and there definitely shouldn't be any anxiety or fear about talking to the other person about their feelings."

Again, I raise a pointed brow. Apparently, Annie is good at doling out advice, but not taking it. "So you're saying that this person should walk away?"

"No, I'm saying that if you feel something for this man, tell him. Men are notoriously aloof. Unless you tell them straight up how you're feeling, most of them won't get it."

Our gazes meet and an understanding passes between us. She knows we're talking about me, and I know that she will have questions for me later. When that happens, I plan to use her advice against her, and she knows that, too.

"I need to get moving. I have class today." With practiced ease, I stand and walk to the door. Annie follows and leans against the jamb as I step into the hall.

"So who is this mystery man?"

I feel a smile inch across my face at the nickname I had used for Ransom before I learned his real name. "I'm afraid I have to plead the fifth."

Her brows arch into her hairline. "Is he a secret agent? FBI? CIA? "

"If only he were so cool," I chuckle as I begin walking away.

"For what it's worth," she says, sticking her head out the door. "I hope it works out for you two. Just remember what I said—*talk to him*. Tell him how you feel. If it's meant to be, it will be."

"You sound like a Disney movie."

"I *am* a princess." She smiles and waves before ducking back into her apartment.

As I walk to my car, her words repeat in my head. She has a point. I need to tell Ransom what's going on in my head. If knowing that I am developing deeper feelings for him scares him away, then I'm better off without him.

I really hope he chooses to stick around, though. There's still so much about Ransom Scott that I aim to explore.

***

Ransom doesn't ask why I was absent yesterday, and as predicted, he doesn't bring up the club or the hotel. The mask he wears is impossible to read. With his dark hair combed back from his forehead and dressed in another pair of khakis and sweater-vest, he's just an unassuming professor—a real nice guy. If I hadn't been there to experience it for myself, I would never guess that little more than thirty-two hours ago we'd had some of the wildest, kinkiest sex I've ever had.

The way he tied me to the bed frame and tore my body asunder makes me shiver just thinking about it. I have a difficult time putting the two images of this man together. He's a prime example of how different people can be in the light of day.

Today, the weather is so nice, Ransom has us working outside. We're gathered on the lawn outside the Art building and he's discussing art history, which is as interesting as it is boring. I think he feels the same way. Twenty minutes ago, he got animated over the Impressionist Movement, and now that he's discussing Modernism. He sounds like he's just repeating the words by rote. It's funny what you can pick up about a person just by observing.

"What I want you to take away from today is that art is everywhere and in countless forms. It's different for everyone," he says as he begins to wrap up his lecture. "When you and I look out over this campus, we see different things. For instance, I see baroque influenced by Roman and Greek design. Maybe you see a series of lines and angles or Victorian landscapes. Think about this as you put together your final exam. How do you plan to use your environment to influence others' visions?"

My mind scrambles. I have no idea what he's talking about, but I am ready to skedaddle. I have a ton of homework ahead of me, and I still have no clue what I'm going to do for my final assignment for this class. He dismisses us and I hurry to finish my notes, and then tuck my books into the crook of my elbow. As I turn to leave, I hear Ransom's throaty timber call me back.

Waiting for the rest of the students to clear out, I take my time approaching him. "I hope this isn't becoming a habit," I say in false warning to help ease the tension I feel inside. "People might start talking."

The corner of Ransom's mouth quirks up. "You weren't in class yesterday."

"I was taking care of a sick friend. Should I have brought a note?"

His smile grows deeper with my sarcasm. "Does this have anything to do with Miss Guerra's absence?"

I nod.

His eyes hold mine for a moment longer than is comfortable. His voice is quiet and filled with concern when he says, "I just wanted to make sure you were okay, and that, uh..." He clears his throat, and the sudden nervous energy he gives off has me curious. "The kiss. I wanted to make sure it didn't... scare you."

I study him for a moment, the tightness around his eyes and the firm line of his lips. I remember that kiss fondly. How gentle he was, how sweet it felt. But it makes no sense to ask me this, considering all we did to one another after that. Unless he's still worried about how this will affect our personal and professional lives.

I consider this. "No," I whisper, my voice growing deeper as the memories of that kiss plays through my mind on repeat. "Are you?"

His gaze glued to my mouth, he shakes his head slowly. "At first. I have a lot to lose, but I haven't stopped thinking about it for a second. Your mouth…"

He trails off, and when I glance down, I see the evidence of how much that memory affects him. His words are like the first move on a chess board, and it gives me the confidence to make the second move.

Maintaining a careful and respectful distance, I take a step closer, lowering my voice so no one else can hear. "If I thought I could get away with it, I'd drop to my knees right now and show you *exactly* what this mouth can do, *Mr. Scott.*"

He sucks air in sharply through his teeth and draws back. The flames of desire in his eyes blazes back at me. In a single, hard blink, he banks it. Shaking his head, Ransom takes a step back. "You should go now, Miss Hart, before something bad happens."

I smirk because I knew he'd be the one to draw the line. I wonder if he realizes how transparent he is. Carefully Controlled Mr. Scott by day is nothing like Uninhibited Mr. Scott by night. "Afraid someone will catch us?"

His chest is pressed against mine in an instant, heat rolling off him in waves. With his lips against my ear, he growls, "The only thing I'm afraid of is that I'll lose control and shove my cock so far down your throat, you'll choke on it."

Holy shit. The smile falls from my face at the mental image, replaced with a near-crippling desire to drop before him and taste his hard flesh between my lips. As it turns out, it's me who draws the line.

"I should go," I say thickly, because someone has to be the voice of reason, before we both end up in trouble.

He watches me as I back away with a mocking smile. "Yes, you certainly should."

Eleven

I've managed to stay away for a solid week. Having a class with Ransom makes this a nearly impossible feat—like reaching the summit of Mount Everest without a guide and lacking any survival skills.

To keep myself busy, and my mind off anything having to do with him, I throw myself into my studies. On the days I have to work, I use dancing to distract myself, which is also harder than hell, because every few minutes I find myself searching the corners for a pair of familiar dark eyes.

Thankfully, Ransom keeps his distance, too. I don't know if he was trying to scare me off, but it works—kind of. Try as I might, I can't stop thinking about him, about the kiss, the sex. Everything. He completely dominates my every thought. There's no escape.

It's driving me crazy, wanting to touch him, but forcing myself to stay away. It's better for both of us this way. At least, that's what I keep telling myself. I just wish I didn't have to see his face every day.

That's why I've ditched yoga for running. I've found that it helps me clear my head far better than the downward facing dog. For just a little while, I can get lost in the steady rhythm of my feet slapping the pavement and the whirring of my breaths in my ears.

I don't have a lot of stamina, but I can get a good mile in before I have to take a break. This morning, I hit the streets early while it's still cool enough out to break a comfortable sweat. The path I take circles the campus. I pass a couple runners while I'm out, but it's still pretty early, which means I have the trail mostly to myself.

I am coming up on the half-mile marker when someone falls into step beside me. Focused on the music between my ears and the sidewalk stretched out ahead, the interruption startles me and I misstep, nearly falling on my face.

"Whoa, careful there, grace."

Ripping the bud from my ear, I glare up at Ransom. "You scared the hell out of me!"

Grinning in amusement, he holds his hands up in front of him. "I'm sorry, I didn't mean to. I was just out for a run when I saw you. I didn't know you ran."

"I just started," I grumble.

His gaze drifts down my body, and I can't help feeling a little self-conscious. I don't have any makeup on, I'm sweaty, and I probably stink. "Yeah? How far do you go?"

"Up to the dorms. About a mile or so."

He looks ahead thoughtfully. "You could do more," he decides.

I shake my head in annoyance. "No, I can't. I just started. I need time to build up stamina."

"You were going pretty hard. It took me a minute to catch up with you. If you slowed down a bit, you'd be able to hold out longer. Plus, it's less wear and tear on your knees."

I mull over this as I catch my breath. "Thanks for the advice. I'll keep it in mind. I should get back to it though before my heart rate gets too low."

"Mind if I run with you?"

I do, actually, but it's hard to deny him when he's looking at me like that, as if he's hoping I'll say yes, but worried I'll say no. I want to turn him down. The voice in my head is telling me if I don't walk away now, this last week will have been for nothing, but I find myself inclining my head and saying, "If you think you can keep up with me."

His smirk is paralyzing. "I'll do my best."

We fall into a comfortable silence as we run side by side. The pace that Ransom sets is slower than my usual, but I find it's easier to breathe when my heart isn't slamming against my ribcage, and by the end of our run, we've covered a good two and a half miles, a whole one and a half more than my usual.

I'm out of breath when we stop at the end of campus, and my mouth is drier than the desert on a sunny afternoon, but I feel great. I feel healthy and my head is clear. I don't know if that's because the object of my obsession is standing beside me, or if it's because I'm too tired to think, but it's refreshing nonetheless.

I'm surprised to realize that running with Ransom wasn't such a challenge after all. It was actually kind of fun. Even though we didn't talk about anything, it was nice to have someone else to share it with. I'm not ready to let that feeling go just yet. There's a little coffee shop at the end of the block and I am about to ask him if he wants to grab a cup with me, when Ransom speaks up.

"I need to get back and grab a shower. It was nice running into you. We should do it again sometime."

"Oh, yeah, sure. Maybe tomorrow morning...if you're out, because I will be. Running, that is." I stumble over my words, feeling like a complete idiot because of how pathetic I sound.

The corners of his mouth tilt up. He steps into me, his hand covering my clammy arm, and kisses my cheek. "Sure thing, Hart. Same time and place." As soon as I nod in agreement, he turns and heads off in the opposite direction, leaving me standing in the middle of the sidewalk wearing a ridiculous grin that I can't seem to wipe off my face.

***

Annie is waiting for me when I get to class, which means I am back to sitting front and center. Having gotten used to being in the back of the room, the change is difficult to get used to. I feel exposed, vulnerable.

And Ransom's concerted effort to avoid me makes me feel all the more conspicuous because instead of being invisible, I can *feel* how aware he is of me. Maybe the problem is that I am focusing too hard on *him*, but I can't help it. Does the man have to be so damn irresistible?

This pattern continues into the following week. By now, it's becoming old hat. He's also stopped coming to the club, which is both a relief and a disappointment. I'm never certain how to read him, but the distance we've placed between us seems to finally be sticking. I have to admit, it's getting easier to be around him. Each day that passes without incident is a little less torturous than the last. Now, I'd venture to say we're almost comfortable in each other's presence. Ransom's even taken to speaking directly to me, and I'm learning to get a handle on the furious blush that constantly wants to seep into my face every time he does.

It's Friday and we've just finished discussing religion in art, when Annie raises her hand.

Ransom points to her. "I have a question about my final assignment."

He nods as he closes his book and gathers his papers. "Meet me at my desk after class."

Great. Right now, I'd like more than anything to punch Annie a good one, because I know she will expect me to stay after with her, and that is exactly the kind of attention I am trying to avoid. We're just beginning to learn to work within the same space, so the last thing Ransom and I need is more one-on-one time.

As the class files out moments later, I try my luck and give Annie a quick pat on the shoulder and issue an even quicker, "See you later." But she grabs my elbow before I can get far, and pulls me back.

"Wait for me. I'll just be a minute."

Grumbling, I stand aside, eying the open door. My mind cycles through possible escape plans, but even having taken up running and pushing three miles a day won't be enough to outrun the devil, which is exactly what Annie will turn into if I bolt. The girl is terrifying when she's angry.

"I was thinking about this," Annie says as she hands something over to Ransom. From where I stand, I can't see what it is that she shows him, but whatever it is, he seems interested.

"This is good. It's risky, definitely controversial, but if you're up to the challenge, then I say go for it."

My interest is piqued. Even though several feet still separate us, I lean closer. I still can't see a damn thing, but I do catch the look on Annie's face. It's one of doubt, which is at total odds with Ransom's expression.

"Okay, thanks, Professor Scott." We walk out together. Annie remains tight-lipped all the way out the doors, until the anticipation becomes too much and I decide to pull answers out of her.

"Okay, talk. What was that about back there?"

She shrugs. "Nothing. Just an idea I was tossing around for the final project. I don't know if I'm going to do it, though. Like Professor Scott said, it's kind of risky."

"How risky?" Annie isn't the kind of person I would describe as a risk taker. In fact, she's ultraconservative. The only risk I've ever witnessed her take is mixing darks with lights.

Instead of answering with words, she pulls a scrap of paper from inside the folder she carries between a stack of books and hands it over. It has the name of the school stamped at the top and I realize that it is an article that has been torn from the monthly newsletter that circulates campus.

As I read it over, my eyes grow wide. Shock fills my voice and I screech to a halt, turning on Annie, who's chewing nervously on her bottom lip. "You're going to *pose nude*?"

Several people on the quad glance at us, but continue walking. Annie clutches her books to her chest, growing pale. "I don't know. The more I think about it, the more I think it's a stupid idea.

I mean, I still wear a shirt when I have sex, and I've been with Jason for years."

I can see where that could be a problem. I don't want to discourage my friend from taking chances, but this is the kind that I know she will regret. Friends don't let friends make bad choices. "Sweetie, this is so not you."

"I know." She sighs, defeated. "I just thought it could be an easy A. Take my clothes off for an hour, let some people draw me, and then go."

"Trust me," I say as we resume walking. "Taking your clothes off for strangers isn't as easy as it might sound. If you can't do it for your boyfriend, then you definitely aren't ready to do it for anyone else."

She nods thoughtfully, and I know she's hearing me. But I also know that even if I hadn't said anything, she would have reached the same conclusion. Annie is smart that way. If she isn't comfortable with something, then she steers clear of it. Which is why it's so damn hard for me to understand why she chose the boyfriend she did.

"Have you decided what you're going to do for your project?" she asks me.

"Nope. Then again," I say, bumping her shoulder with mine, "maybe I'll go pose nude in your stead."

"Maybe you should," she says, shocking me. "You've got the body for it, and I know you're not shy."

"I feel like I should be offended," I tease.

"No, not at all. You're just a heck of a lot more confident than I am. You should give it some serious consideration. And you never know, maybe that mystery man of yours will get jealous of all those people seeing what belongs to him, and drag you out of there by your hair like a total caveman."

"Oh, yes, because I've always wanted my very own caveman. Those bulbous foreheads and ape-ish good looks make me weak in the knees."

We laugh, but the closer we get to the parking lot, the more I consider her suggestion. My relationship with Ransom aside, it would be an excellent opportunity, and she's right. Thanks to stripping, I don't have any issue with showing my body to strangers. That ship's sailed. It could be a chance to get a good final grade with unforeseen benefits.

Tucking the article in my pocket, I promise myself I will think more about it later. "So, who's up for drinks tonight?"

Twelve

Music hums from the two-story colonial as Annie and I make our way up the sidewalk. People spill from the open door onto the large porch and into the front yard. After pulling a short shift after class, I'm ready to party.

Our usual fare is to meet up with friends at a bar, get shitfaced, and sing bad karaoke, but tonight is different. Brody and his Greek brothers are elevating a few lucky pledges to full members of the fraternity, and it's a cause for celebration. So, here we are.

The moment we cross the threshold, I'm questioning the wisdom of being here. Half the student body seems to have crammed itself into what is probably a normally large space. Total chaos appears to be the theme they've gone with. Random panties and bras hang from lampshades and chandeliers. A girl crouches in the corner, emptying her stomach into a potted plant. There's a guy walking around with a trash bag, his attempt to keep some kind of order feeble at best—he must be a pledge.

Someone shouts, and then everyone erupts into excited cheers. Annie and I try to make ourselves small as the crowd parts down the middle and a group of guys wearing togas race by, blasting each other with water balloons.

The place is a zoo. Annie and I share a look. "I'm going to get something to drink."

"Jason said he was here. I'm going to go see if I can find him."

"Okay. I have my phone on. Text me if you need me." That's our plan. Whenever we find ourselves in a scene like this, we keep our phones on. If one of us gets into trouble, or just needs to check in, we're only a text or call away.

Annie's expression is strained as she walks away. I watch her go until the crowd swallows her, and then I head for the kitchen. It's located at the back of the house, and when I get there, I let out a low, appreciative whistle.

Someone meant business.

The kitchen is fully stocked. There's a baby pool set up in the middle of the floor and it's packed full of ice and a variety of bottles and cans. There's also a keg, and beyond that, a collection of mixers.

There's a line for the keg, and there're too many people collecting at the counter, so I grab the first thing that touches my fingers from the pool. It's a cheap strawberry wine cooler, but I like strawberries and as long as it contains alcohol, then it'll do the job.

My first drink disappears fast and I collect another one before I start searching the house for Brody. I find him in the basement playing football on a large screen television with three other guys. There are girls everywhere, littering the floors and backs of the furniture. When they see me coming, a couple of them eye me with suspicion.

I recognize their type immediately. They're like buzzards, hovering on the outskirts, hoping a few scraps will be tossed their way. When I lean over the back of the couch and wrap my arms around Brody's neck, I catch the eye of a girl standing across the room.

She's pretty, with blonde hair, light eyes, tall and skinny—the total opposite of me. Her glare would be piercing if I gave a damn, but I don't. When Brody tilts his head back and realizes it's me, his smile is so brilliant, everyone in the room vanishes.

"J, you made it!"

Jumping to his feet, he spins and grabs me around the waist. With both of his massive arms, he pulls me over the back of the couch. I scream in surprise, gripping his shoulders for dear life, but then he's crushing me against his muscled chest, and I have to concentrate all my energy on breathing.

"Did you get anything to drink?" he asks, pointing to a table littered with unopened beers. Apparently, the floor is where the empties go.

"Dude, you just got sacked!"

"You're supposed to pause it, numbnuts!"

I shake my head as Brody pulls me down onto his knee and grabs his controller. I can feel eyes on me, and I know it's from the other girls. I focus on the television, laughing to myself. If any of them knew how unromantic my relationship is with Brody, they wouldn't need to feel threatened. After I leave here tonight, there is no doubt in my mind that one of them will be occupying his bed.

I zone out as I watch the guys play. Brody wins every round, which he thanks me for with a kiss on the cheek every time. Apparently, I'm his good luck charm.

"I call foul," one of the guys that I recognize from a couple classes complains. He drops his controller on the floor and slumps into the chair, a lock of brown hair falling over his forehead. Immediately, his lap is filled by a pretty brunette flashing way too much cleavage.

"For what?" Brody chuckles as he settles back against the cushions, taking me with him.

"You had Lady Luck on your side; ergo, it wasn't a fair match."

"He's right. I call for a rematch!"

"You can't call for a rematch, Trent," Brody says, his chest rumbling with laughter. "Should have come prepared."

"I thought this was supposed to be a friendly game," Trent says. "Had I known how cutthroat you are, I would have brought along my own golden snatch."

Brody's fist flies so fast and hard into Trent's shoulder that I nearly topple off his lap. He catches me at the last possible second, and I glimpse the apology that flickers in his eyes before he's focused on the guy behind me. "Watch your mouth."

"You'd better listen to the man," football guy says with a cocky smirk. "Brody'll rip your limbs off and beat you with them if you talk bad about his lady."

"Dude, I wasn't," Trent says, his eyes growing wide. Rubbing his arm, he sends Brody a pleading look. "I didn't mean anything by it, man."

"Whatever. Just watch your mouth," he growls. Tapping my thigh, I take his cue and stand. Brody's right there beside me, his arm winding around my shoulders as he leads me back up the stairs. "I'll catch up with you scumbags later."

Brody takes me on a loop through the first floor. After getting a fresh pair of drinks, I figure he's going to take me outside for some air, but I find myself climbing the stairs instead.

"Where are you taking me?" I ask as I step over a girl who's passed out in the middle of the staircase. "Is she okay?"

"She's fine," he mutters. He leads us past several closed doors, a few of which emit some questionable noises. Pushing one open, I hold my breath, unsure what I'll find on the other side, only to see a dark, quiet room.

He closes the door behind us, and it's as if we've entered a whole new realm. The level of noise downstairs compared to the utter silence here makes it feel as though I've stuffed cotton in my ears.

"Is this your room?" I ask, taking a look around. I've never seen it before—like I said, we're just friends—and I take a moment to assess my surroundings. It's small with light gray walls. There are a couple of school flags pinned to the wall over a simple pine dresser, clothes spilling out of the open drawers. A few pairs of shoes are piled up behind the door, and Brody kicks off the pair he is wearing adding them to the top.

"Yep," he says, and crashes face-first onto the unmade, full-sized bed.

"It's…tidy. For a guy." Toeing off my own shoes, I climb onto the bed and stretch out beside him. Then, I jump back up. "I'm not sitting in your cum am I?"

His shoulders shake with silent laughter and he rolls his head to the side to look up at me. "Relax, the sheets were washed earlier this week." I give him a pointed look, because it's been almost a full week, and I know how fast guys work. He rolls his eyes. "Come on, J. Even I don't work that fast."

Following his recommendation, I relax. "So, what are we doing in here?"

"Escaping," he says.

"Why? You looked like you were having fun."

Folding his arms under his cheek, he stares blankly at my crossed legs. "I was, but it's nicer up here. It's quiet."

The music pounds through the floor, but after a few drinks, its rhythmic beat is almost soothing. "Are you drunk?"

One side of his face creases, showing off a shallow dimple. "Maybe a little." His expression smoothes out and he reaches out to lay his hand on my shin. "Thanks for coming tonight."

"Anything for you," I say honestly, because it's the truth. He and Annie are the only people in my life who've earned that distinction, and it's because I know they feel the same about me.

"Is that right?" His honey-brown eyes gleam wickedly as he pushes up onto all fours and prowls toward me.

I stiffen because I'm not stupid. Brody loves me, and not always in a friendly way. He usually hides it well, but I've caught glimpses of it in the rare moments that he let his guard down. It's even more apparent when he's been drinking, like tonight. I've never brought it up to him because it will change everything. But it means I always have my eye out looking for warning signs.

This is a warning sign if ever I've seen one.

"What are you up to?" I ask with a tight smile, attempting to play off the anxiety that's beginning to build. *Please don't make this awkward.* The last thing I want to do is hurt him.

"How long have we known each other?" he asks, now hovering over me.

I have to tilt my head back to look into his eyes. Whatever he's thinking, I can't read him. "I don't know. A few years. Why?"

He stares me down, his brown eyes holding mine and I end up holding my breath for so long I grow lightheaded. I don't know what he planned to say, but I see in his eyes the moment he decides to go in another direction. His full lips inch up into a crooked grin. "Because you've never given me a massage."

I bounce as he shifts his weight and drops down on the bed beside me. "Rub me, woman," he says into the pillow.

Finally, my lungs inflate, and I feel a huge weight lifted. I know that's not what he was going to say, but I'm so glad he did. Less complication, that's what I need in my life right now.

Throwing my leg over his hips, I straddle him. "Hard, or soft?"

There's a pause, and I can almost hear the wheels turning in his head as he tries to decide how to answer the question. His voice thick, he says, "Any way you want it."

Thirteen

"The man is in love with you."

Annie is the voice of reason. Always has been. But that doesn't mean I have to like what she says. I hate when she's right. "I know, but I can't be what he wants me to be."

"Why not? You've known each other for, like, ever. Longer than we've been friends. Isn't there some kind of unwritten rule about this sort of thing? If you're friends with someone of the opposite sex for more than five years, you have to get married?"

I wrinkle my nose as I chase a grape tomato around my plate. First thing I did after rolling out of bed this morning was call Annie and asked her to join me for lunch to catch up on last night's party. I intended to find out about the status between her and Jason, but the conversation ended up being focused on me and my love life instead.

I shake my head, unsure how I got myself into this.

"I don't think that exists," I tell her.

"Well, then, it should. You two would make a cute couple."

I don't bother to respond. Cute couple or not, I just don't look at Brody that way. Maybe if we hadn't been friends first, but we were and we are and I just can't see risking it all for a *chance* that it could turn into something more. I have few enough people in my life as it is.

"What about this other guy, the one you're seeing. Did you talk to him yet?"

"No," I admit, "but I think it's run its course."

The looks she gives me is full of apologies. "That sucks, hun. You mentioned that it was complicated between you two. Like a forbidden thing? Does that mean you still have to see him around?"

"Every day." And it doesn't suck as much as I thought it would. I may not get to be as close to Ransom as I want to, but he hasn't been completely cut from my life. I'm not sure if it would have been better to have a clean break, but this arrangement feels manageable. It's better than nothing, anyway.

"Gah, I can't even imagine. Isn't that hard? I mean, do you ever feel like you're going to lose your mind if you can't touch him?"

All the time. "Not really. We weren't in love or anything." *I might have been in love.*

I really wish she'd drop the subject, but I can tell by the flashes of excitement in her eyes that Annie is just getting started.

"Okay, you know I have to ask," she says, holding her hands up in front of her in a stop motion. "Do I know him?"

I pack what's left of my salad into my mouth to bide me some time to think. Revealing my relationship with Ransom could be a bad idea. But then again, our relationship is past tense. How dangerous could it be? Plus, this is Annie we're talking about here. Being my best friend, she's bound by the laws of friendship to take my secrets to the grave.

I hesitate. "Um… kind of, yeah."

Her eyes grow even wider and she leans over the table, her hands coming down to grip my wrists. "Oh…my…God. Tell me!" she whispers. "Is it the English professor? Professor Hale? He's so hot. I break into a sweat every time I go to his class."

TMI. I laugh uncomfortably because she's closer to the truth than she realizes. "No, although, he is pretty sexy." Professor Hale is only a couple years older than us and has dark brown hair, deep, soulful eyes, and a perpetual five o'clock shadow. Who wouldn't love that combination?

"Heck yeah, he is!" She grows quiet again, her gaze holding mine as if she's trying to pluck the information out of my head. Then she starts rattling off the names of every guy we've ever run into, from Billy, the bartender at DJ's, to some guy I went out on one date with two years ago. When she's exhausted all her options, her look turns pleading.

"Just *tell me*," she hisses, desperate for information. "I swear on a stack of Holy Bibles I won't tell a soul." I sip my soda, making her tough it out a little longer. "If you're not going to tell me, then please just shoot me and put me out of my misery."

I laugh, and then decide *what's the worst that could happen?* Leaning in, I make sure to keep my voice low so no one overhears us. "It's...Professor Scott."

"No!"

"Yes." I nod.

"No way!"

"Yes way."

She sits back, stunned for a few minutes, and now that the cat is out of the bag we let it marinate. Finally, she blinks a few times, takes a drink of her soda, and gives me a look that tells me I'm not going to like what she's about to say. "I hope you know that you have to pose nude now."

***

Annie is relentless. She's buzzing in my ear every chance she gets about signing up for the nude art program. I'll admit that I'm intrigued by the concept, and even briefly considered it a possibility, but the more she pressures me, the less sure I become.

What if I know someone there? The main reason I've been able to dance at all is because I've never run into anyone—save Ransom—that I know. The anonymity is crucial, which is the purpose of the type of lighting I've chosen. If it ever happens to chance that someone I do know is in the audience, at least I won't know about it.

Annie's push to get me to do this just reinforces that fear. If I pose, then someone is going to recognize me, whether from before or after the class. And then what do I do?

Yet, even though I'm resisting, I still don't have the first clue what I'm going to do for my final project. To be honest, I haven't even given it any serious thought. I won't lie. Having one ready to go fall into my lap is tempting.

As the week progresses, I watch each of my classmates add their name to the list Ransom posted declaring their final project. Between classes and work and dealing with questions surrounding my love life, I'm so exhausted, I can't think straight, and the pressure is beginning to set in.

Which is why, when I find myself walking into Mrs. Jackson's art lab Wednesday morning, I blame everything on Annie.

I find Mrs. Jackson behind an easel working diligently. She's not like the other teachers. Her red hair is a few shades too bright to be real, her clothes too eclectic to be conservative, and the tattoos decorating one arm too *everything* to truly fit in with the rest of the professors. But that's probably the point. She's declared herself a misfit, and I take an immediate liking to her.

When she sees me come in, she sets down her paintbrush and wipes her hands off on a paper towel. "Are you here for the sculpting class?"

"Um, no." My smile is faint. I'm not used to feeling so nervous, especially when fully clothed. "I was wondering if the spot for the model is still open."

Her look turns questioning before a sudden smile spills across her face. "Oh, the nude model. Yes, yes, come on in." She waves for me to follow her to her desk, where she hands me a clipboard and a pen. "You're just in time. We only have a few slots left."

My hand trembles and I talk myself out of doing this a half-dozen times as I fill in my name at the bottom of the paper. This is such a bad idea. Why am I doing this? Oh, yeah. Annie. I'm blaming it all on Annie. "There are a lot of names on there," I comment as I slide the clipboard back across her desk. Thankfully, I don't recognize any of them.

Her smile grows wider. "Yes, it's a very popular program. Unfortunately, we had to cut back on participants this year."

"Why's that?" I ask curiously as we begin slowly walking back toward the door.

"The university cut funding to some of the programs this year. As this is one of the few paying gigs on campus, it was one of the first on the chopping block."

Stopping in my tracks, I turn to her. "Paying gig?"

"Yes." Her head cants to the side, and she frowns. "Each model gets a hundred dollars for their time and a gift certificate to Jed's."

So free dinner and cash. Suddenly, my earlier concerns don't seem as pressing.

"You didn't know?"

I shake my head. "I had no idea."

"Well, I'm sure now that you do it takes some of the scariness out of it."

I grin. "That's very true."

"Do you have any questions for me?"

"None that I can think of." But I do have the sudden urge to give Annie a hug and thank her for pushing me. "Thanks for your time."

"No problem. Enjoy your evening."

I rush home in a better mood than I've been in weeks. The boost of adrenalin gets me through a full night of work and even earns me extra tips. The high carries over into the next day, too. Something Ransom seems to pick up on. He smiles more, directs more of his attention to my side of the room. Even Annie notices, nudging me each time he does it.

Maybe she was paying a little too close attention, though, or I wasn't paying enough attention to her. I might have seen that she was up to something, but I didn't. When she lingers after class, I figure she has another question to ask about an assignment.

I don't expect her to ask Ransom out.

"It's just a little get-together with friends. Nothing fancy."

Ransom casts a brief look at me over her shoulder, and I try to communicate my extreme dislike of this turn of events, but he doesn't seem to notice. Thankfully, he's on the same page. "I'm sorry, Miss Guerra, I appreciate the offer, but it's probably best if I don't."

"Is this because you're a teacher? Because you've gotta eat, right? If anyone asks, we can tell them it's a study group."

He cocks an eyebrow. "A study group. At a bar."

"Of course. It would be incredibly inappropriate to hold it at your house. This is a public place. No one could question your intent."

I completely disagree with her. I doubt if the dean or someone higher up saw one of the instructors sharing drinks with the student body that they'd look very highly on it.

"I still think I'd better take a pass," Ransom insists, and I breathe a sigh of relief.

"Well, we'll save a seat just in case you change your mind," Annie presses on. "Even professors have to eat."

Ransom and I share a look as Annie breezes by me on her way out the door. Mine is a warning that he'd better not show up tonight. I don't know what his is.

The second I step outside, I grab Annie's elbow and wheel her around. "What are you doing?"

Her smile is devious. It knocks me back a step because nothing about Annie is devious. At least, I never thought it was. "You might claim that it's done between you two, but I know better. I don't know how I never noticed it before, but you two are totally in love!"

My head snaps back and my nose scrunches at the accusation. "We are not!"

"Are too! You two can't keep your eyes off each other. I swear, even with air conditioning, it was a sauna in there today. Hell, you practically burned my clothes off."

"Now you're just exaggerating." This is the Annie everyone fears. When she gets feisty like this, it's usually best if everyone gives in or walks away. I'm about to walk away.

"I'm right. You give him the same look Brody gives you. Admit it, you still want him."

"No." My jaw clenches and I walk faster. Only two hundred and two steps until I reach my car.

"Admit it!" Annie has to practically jog to keep up because of her short legs.

"Fuck you!" I snarl and pick up the pace until *she's* jogging. But whatever fuel she's running on today is allowing her to keep up, which isn't good for me. I round on her, irritated and desperate for her to leave me alone. I've closed this chapter. I don't need her trying to pry it open.

"What do you want me to say?" I yell at her.

She isn't even fazed by my anger. "Just admit that you're still into him."

My eyes narrow on her. I hate this side of Annie. I hate that she makes me look at myself, question myself. Casting my gaze around the parking lot, I reluctantly give her what she wants. "Fine, I'm still into him. But," I add, cutting off her clapping and delighted squeal, "that doesn't mean that I'm going after him. It's over."

"I hear you," she claims, but there's something about the way she says it that makes me suspicious. "I have to run. We're meeting at eight tonight, right?"

I still don't trust her, but I nod. "Brody said he reserved a table."

"Great! I'm bringing Jason. See you there."

A night out with friends and Jason. All I can say is that the guy had better be on his best behavior. Assuming he manages to actually show up.

Fourteen

I spent way too much time picking an outfit, and now I'm late. Jed's is packed for a weeknight, but Brody's ability to plan ahead allows me to go straight in. The hostess points me toward a table in the back, and even though I spent the entire afternoon filled with doubt and a creeping sense of unease due to Annie's strange behavior, I still find myself searching for any sign of Ransom.

I hate myself for being so weak. Why can't I just stop thinking about him? I need a distraction, something to help me take my mind off everything. I feel some of the tension I've been carrying around when I spot everyone seated around the table. Brody brought a couple of his friends along, as well as Mitch and Price, who we've known for years, and I see that Annie managed to drag Jason along, too. I can't say that I'm happy to see his blotchy red face, but I am happy that Annie appears happy.

Brody sees me first, and his wide smile serves an injection of happy. I could be in the worst mood, and one look at him would make everything right again.

Maybe Annie was onto something. Why am I chasing after someone untouchable, when I have Brody?

That's an easy question to answer. It's the very fact that Ransom is untouchable that makes me crave him. I've always been the kind of person who gravitated toward trouble. A shrink would probably tell me that I have daddy issues, or it's due to my parents' untimely deaths and having to grow up too fast. And they'd be right because what kind of person could get dealt the hand I have and not be screwed up?

Unfortunately, I can't help wanting what I want. The side effect of owning a heart is that you can't control who it falls for. There's no reasoning with it, no talking it out of stupid decisions. Even when it's bound to get burned, it runs headlong into the fire. But people can train themselves to like different things. Can't they?

When Brody leaves the table and embraces me, I decide to prove to my heart that it doesn't rule me, and I give him an extra-long hug. His arms tighten around my shoulders and he kisses my hair in response. When he pulls back, he gives me a strange smile like he's not quite sure what to make of my behavior. Hell, neither am I. I just know that I need to crush this unhealthy obsession for Ransom before it takes over any more of my life.

After forcing his friends to move down so I can have the chair directly beside him, Brody pours me a glass of beer from the pitcher sitting in the center of the table.

"You look beautiful tonight," he says, leaning down to whisper the compliment in my ear.

"As opposed to every other night?"

The kiss he places on my temple is sweet and full of affection. "You know what I meant."

I do. Brody always appreciates the way I look, even when I'm at my worst. Finding his heavy thigh under the table, I squeeze it. "Thanks."

His eyes catch mine, and he tips his head. It would be so easy to let myself fall for him. Brody is an easy guy to love. He's charming and sweet, cute and gentle, and the best part of all— we're friends. We don't even have to try to get along because the connection is already there.

Laying my head on his shoulder, I glance down the table to where Annie and Jason are seated. She's looking at me with raised brows, and I raise mine right back. I don't know what message she's trying to send me, but I hope she gets mine—I don't need anyone's approval on how I choose to live my life.

"Good to see you made it, Jason," I say, raising my voice so he can hear me over the music. "We missed you last time."

He lifts his chin, a gesture I've always hated, but only when he does it. "Hey, Joe."

That's about the extent of our exchange. Jason and I used to get along, almost like friends. He was cool, someone I could laugh and joke around with. Then I found out what he was really about. Not wanting to cause trouble or hurt anyone, I distanced myself, but when I saw how his behavior was affecting Annie, Jason and I had a heart-to-heart. It didn't go well, and Annie still doesn't know anything about it, but, needless to say, Jason and I will never be friends.

The waitress arrives with two platters piled high with appetizers and sets them down in the middle of the table, along with plates for everyone. Brody fills mine first, and my eyes widen at the amount of food he gives me.

"I can't eat all this." Hell, I can't even see the plate.

"I'll eat what you don't," he says, smiling as he chews on a chili-covered fry.

"That's why he did it," Mitch says. He's seated across from Brody, and his hazel eyes twinkle with mirth. "I bet half the food on your plate is intended for him. He just wants to make sure none of us get any."

Brody pats his flat stomach and grins shamelessly as he chews a stuffed potato. "I'm a growing boy."

"That's nothing. You should see him at breakfast," the one who vacated his seat for me says. I think his name is Trent. "If you're not first at the table, there's a good chance you won't eat."

"This is how it starts," Mitch says, shaking his head. "A little extra fries here, and a couple more chips there. Before you know it, you've become his unwilling partner in crime while all your friends go hungry."

I cover my mouth to keep the beer from coming back out as I laugh. "Who says I'm unwilling?"

Mitch's jaw drops and Brody belts out a laugh as he slings his arm over my shoulder. "Yeah, Mitch, who says she's unwilling?"

Spending time with my friends is always cathartic. The next couple hours pass fast, with a lot of food and even more drinks shared among us. Brody always finds a way to touch me, whether it's brushing my hair off my shoulder or putting his arm around the back of my chair and absently tracing his fingers down my arm. By the time our empty plates are taken away, he's given up trying to keep up any pretenses of being just friends, and pulls me into his lap.

I don't mind. We've always been close, and I love Brody's affectionate side. It's always there, but it's way more intense when he's been drinking.

Resting my cheek on top of his head, I push my toe into the floor, rocking us gently to the music as we watch our friends dance.

"Do you want to dance with me?"

Closing my eyes, I shake my head. "I like it right here." The truth is, I'm so tired I could fall asleep right now. That's what alcohol does for me, makes me sleepy.

"Brody cinches his arms around my waist, pulling me in tighter to his chest. "Me, too. Your boobs make amazing pillows."

Jerking back, I slap his chest. "Ass!"

"What? They do. They're like little fluffy clouds of heaven."

I slap him again. "My boobs are not little."

He chuckles, pulling me back so he can nuzzle his scruffy cheek against my cleavage. "Nope, they're not. They're exactly the right size." He hums contentedly, and I feel a little...weird letting him get this close.

The line of friendship is vanishing too fast.

Patting his shoulder, I tell him, "It's getting pretty late. Maybe we should round everyone up and say goodnight."

His glassy eyes scan the room. "Yeah, good idea. I'll drive you home."

"No," I say pushing him back in the chair when he attempts to stand. "You've had too much to drink tonight. I'll bring everyone back here, and then *I'll* take *you* home."

When I stand, my head feels a little lighter than usual like it's not fully attached to my body, but it's nothing I haven't experienced before. I'm not a lightweight, but I may have had slightly more to drink tonight than I realized. Still, as I collect everyone and we say our goodbyes, I don't feel unclear. In fact, I feel pretty steady.

I allow Brody to lean against me as I lead him to my car, despite him being more than twice my height and weight. The fact that I can do that without falling over adds to my confidence that I am well enough to drive. When I trip over a crack in the parking lot as I head back to the driver's side, I'm a little less certain, but Brody's house is only five minutes down the road, and my apartment is only a few more from there. All I have to do is take a little extra care in making sure my attention is on the road.

I don't even get the door open when I feel a hand on my shoulder pulling me back.

"There's no way in hell you're getting behind that wheel."

When I look up, it's into Ransom's seriously pissed off, hard as stone onyx eyes. I'm instantly incensed by his presence. What the hell is he doing here? "Excuse me?"

"Give me the keys. I'll drive you two home."

"What makes you think I'll just hand my keys over?"

Tilting his head to one side, he gives me an impatient look. "I know you've been drinking tonight, and you just tripped over your own feet. If you think I'm going to stand back and let you endanger your life and anyone else's, you're sadly mistaken."

"It was a crack," I shoot back lamely.

"There's no crack, just your clumsy, drunken feet."

I laugh. Like, really laugh, with snorts and everything. "Feet can't get drunk." Okay, maybe he has a point.

He gives me a pointed look, and I know I'm beaten. I hand over my keys without further argument because I'm embarrassed to admit that I'm one of *those* people. The kind that think they're the exception to the rule, and I know if he hadn't been here, I might have hurt someone.

"So what are you doing here? I thought you said you were passing on tonight." After transferring Brody, who is so out of it he's asleep the moment his ass hits the backseat of Ransom's car, I climb into the passenger seat and wait for my answer.

"Like your friend said, a guy's gotta eat." He turns the key in the ignition and pauses. Without looking at me, he adds, "And I might have wanted to see you."

Seriously, I'm pathetic because those were the single best words I've heard all week. I know I'm grinning like a lunatic, and I can't stop myself. Giving me a sidelong look, Ransom returns the smile, and then puts the car into drive.

Brody is passed out cold by the time we reach the frat house, and it takes three of his buddies plus Ransom to get him inside and into bed. I take a moment to pull off his shoes and tuck him in, giving him a kiss on the forehead before I go, because who the hell else is going to do it? After making sure someone will check on him throughout the night, I drive home with Ransom.

"Do you want some coffee?" I ask as he parks in front of my place. I know what I'm asking, but I can't get past the fact that he showed up tonight because of me.

It's risky, but what I should do and what I want to do are two entirely different things. Earlier, I thought it would be wiser to explore my options and not dismiss Brody. Now, I think life is too short to deny myself. I can deny it until I'm blue in the face, and maybe tomorrow I'll resort to old habits and do just that, but tonight I want to live a little. I want to have some fun. And I know without a doubt that Ransom can provide it.

He stares up at the darkened windows as he considers my offer. We both know there is no coffee waiting for either of us behind those doors.

I'm just about to retract my offer to save some face when he turns off the car and pops open his door. "Coffee sounds nice."

Fifteen

Thank God Ransom is on the same page. We barely make it past the front door before we're tearing at each other's clothes. I lost my shoes somewhere near the door, my top between the living room and the kitchen, and my pants outside the bathroom. When Ransom pushes me down on the bed, I'm wearing nothing but a pair of lacy black underwear and bra. He's still fully dressed in his jeans and gunmetal gray button-down shirt. He makes causal sexy in a way no man, I've ever met, can. My stomach flutters in anticipation as he stands between my legs and stares down at me.

"I don't know what I'm doing here," he says, his voice low and rough.

"You're here to fuck me."

His grimace gives me a moment of panic. Did I say something wrong? What if he walks away? I sit up, smoothing my hands up his torso. "Stop thinking so much. You're giving me a headache."

"I'm sorry." His fingers burrow into my hair, tugging at the strands as he makes a tight fist at the back of my head. "I just can't stop thinking about how wrong it is for a teacher to be with a student."

"We're more than that, though." Being involved prior has to count for something, right? "We're adults, Ransom. Do you really think anyone would punish us for being attracted to each other?"

"For acting on it, yes. Definitely." Despite his words, Ransom leans down, pressing me back into the mattress, and kisses the swell of my breasts. If he cares so much about the rules, he's certainly not showing it.

Gripping his biceps, I revel in him, in his touch. It's been so long. "Then we'd better make sure no one finds out."

A growl rumbles in the back of his throat and Ransom surges up, claiming my mouth with a bruising kiss. Our hands move frantically as we remove the rest of the clothing that separates us. Ransom is as eager as I am, but somehow he manages to rein it in.

Moving down my body, he nips at my skin, placing soothing licks after each bite. I look down in shock as he positions his wide shoulders beneath my legs. Reaching down to sift my fingers through his hair, my breathing increases in anticipation of his next move. This is another thing he hasn't done in a while. The last time I asked, he had muttered something about being too impatient to be inside me, and that was that.

Seeing him there now, staring up at me, I can hardly breathe. When he covers me with his mouth, my head slams back into the blankets, and a vicious moan rips from my lips. He circles my clit with his tongue and then laps at my opening. Dragging the flat of his tongue up my slit, he repeats the pattern, lapping, circling, tasting, and teasing. Taking me further than he ever has before. It's a torturous dance that causes all of my muscles to convulse, until I am shaking so hard, I can't tell whether I'm going to come or if I already have.

When his touch becomes too painful to bear, I push his head away. He comes up laughing as he wipes his mouth dry. "What the matter, baby?"

I don't even have enough strength in my muscles to lift my arm to punch him. Hooking my legs around his powerful thighs, I open myself to him. "Shut up and fuck me."

Reaching back, he retrieves a condom lying on top of the blankets I hadn't noticed him put there. After rolling it on, he braces himself above me and flexes his hips. His length is long and hard and stretches me as it slowly enters me.

"Yes, Ransom. It feels so good," I moan breathily as he seats himself fully.

"So do you, Josephine. You feel incredible." His eyes slip shut and he moans as he rocks into me. The slow, steady pace he sets is so unlike the way we usually have sex. Tonight, Ransom is taking his time, and I feel it. I feel everything. This isn't sex. This is making love.

When he hooks his arm under my leg and spreads me open even wider, there is no going back. His pelvis rubs my center just right, and I come undone, splintering apart piece by piece as my orgasm slowly rolls over me like ocean waves breaking against a shore—slow, but with unexpected force. There are no fireworks and my toes don't curl up. I haven't even broken a sweat, but I still feel shattered.

It's the most honest feeling I've ever experienced.

Holding him close, I feel Ransom's muscles straining beneath my hands as he chases his own pleasure. My boobs jiggle and my head bangs against the headboard as he lifts himself to begin moving faster.

I watch as his face contorts and the tendons in his neck stand out in stark relief. His hips surge once more, and then he freezes, going completely still as his lips peel back from his teeth and he releases a tortured sound, before collapsing on top of me.

His heart pounds against my chest as he struggles to catch his breath. My hand strokes his back as the other holds his head to my chest. At this moment, with nothing but the soft sounds of our combined breaths between us, I feel at peace. Having never experienced it before, I have no idea what to do with it. But it's… nice.

The feeling is shattered when Ransom rolls away, and hollowness in my chest begins to take its place. But that space is quickly filled again as he takes me with him. Lying on his back, Ransom tucks me under his side and drapes my arm across his chest. My leg moves up to cover his, and when we are completely wrapped around each other, my chest swells with an emotion I can't name.

Whatever it is, I feel safe here. Protected. Home.

***

A low buzzing lures me from my sleep and I am vaguely aware of Ransom peeling me off him to root around on the floor. The buzzing stops and is followed by his voice, which is soft and a little gruff from sleep. The call is short, and then he is back, crawling into bed beside me.

"Are you awake?" he asks, and I roll away, making a sound of complaint. I'm not a morning person. Never have been, but Ransom is determined to make me one.

Pressing his naked body against my back, I can feel his desire for me to wake up burrowing between my thighs. His warm breath tickles the back of my neck and I tilt my head to feel his lips touch my skin.

"What time do you have to be to class?"

Reaching back to cup his head as he continues to nibble at me, I reply, "Nine."

"Mmmm, then you have twenty minutes to get there."

My eyes fly open and I shoot out of bed. "I'm going to be late!" Spotting him still in bed wearing only his smile, I shout, "Get up! I gotta go!"

Moving to the edge of the bed, he watches me rush around the room collecting clothes from the floor. "I'm all for dedication, especially when you keep bending down like that, but maybe today we should just call in sick and stay in bed." I see that look in his eye, hooded and full of desire, and the offer is almost too tempting to ignore. But for once, reason wins out.

With his clothes in hand, I walk back to him. His knees open and I step between them, draping my hands and his clothes over his shoulders. "As much as I'd love to spend the day in bed with you, you have a job to get to. Besides, both of us absent on the same day? Not a good start if we want to keep this on the down-low."

He releases a heavy sigh and presses his forehead to my sternum. "You're right. God, why do you have to be right?" he complains, throwing his head back and squeezing his eyes shut.

I chuckle and step back, handing him his clothes. "You'd better run if you don't want to be late."

I don a robe as he dresses, and then I walk him to the door. Turning before he leaves, he hooks me around the waist and hauls me up against his chest, dropping a possessive kiss on my lips that leaves me feeling winded. "See you in class, Miss Hart."

I'm smiling like a loon when he opens the door to go, only to have it fall away in an instant. Ransom freezes on the spot. Annie stands on the other side of the door, two coffees in her hand and a look of shock on her face.

Ransom clears his throat. "Good morning, Miss Guerra."

Blinking away her surprise, Annie's expression turns sly as she takes in my appearance. "Good morning, indeed, Professor Scott. Joe, what in the world did I just walk into?"

I rush to explain. "Annie, Professor Scott was just dropping by to…" My excuse dies, and I look to him for help. He is rumpled from head to toe, clearly having just rolled out of bed.

"Uh…tell her about a possible project idea I came across."

"Right," I say, snapping my fingers and pointing at him. "The project."

Annie's suspicious gaze shifts between us, and of course she's not buying it. Even a blind person could see through the lie. "Riiiiight."

"So, okay then. Thanks for the info, Professor Scott. See you in class."

I reach past him and yank Annie by the forearm into the apartment. Ransom gives me a worried look as he exchanges places with her. I don't know what to say or do, so I shrug and close the door in his face. Annie won't tell anyone about this, and I will make sure he knows this when I catch up with him later, but right now, I need to do damage control.

"Thank God you brought coffee!" Relieving her of the extra cup, I gulp it, the hot liquid scalding my tongue on the way down. "You don't even know how much I needed this."

Reclining on my couch, she pulls her feet up on the cushion beside her and gives me a knowing look. "Oh, I can take a guess. How the hell did he end up here? I assume he stayed the night?"

"It's a long story, and yes, he did. Don't," I say firmly as I point my finger at her, "tell anyone. Not even Jason."

She holds up her hand. "I swear, my lips are sealed."

I stare her down for a moment longer, and when I'm satisfied that I've gotten through to her, I nod. "Okay, I'm going to hop in the shower. Be back in five." Her voice floats down the hall after me as I gather what I'll wear for the day—a pair of cut-off shorts, a white tank top, and a black and white checkered button-down that's two sizes too large.

"So, was he good?"

"So good!" I call back as I duck inside the bathroom. Her laughter is drowned out by the rushing water, and as I step beneath it, I realize once again that I can't stop smiling.

Professor Ransom Scott is ruining me.

Sixteen

The good thing about having a job that allows me to afford a place off-campus is having privacy. Ransom ends up spending the night with me over the weekend, which quickly becomes every night the following week. None of which would be possible if I had to worry about sneaking him out of my room every morning. We're spending so much time together outside of class and work now, that I'm not sure how I will ever be able to go back to sleeping alone. He's taken up space in my bed like he's taken up space in my lungs. If we go back to how things were before, I worry I won't be able to breathe without him.

We've also become dedicated running buddies. Between that and our morning sexcapades, I'm getting more cardio than I ever got dancing on a stage. We may not be like an ordinary couple, able to go out and be seen together, but I feel like we're in a good place.

Ransom is different with me—a good different. I still catch glimpses of his dominant side, but his flair for passion has changed. I don't pretend to know what caused it, but he's gentler now, sweeter. He treats me with care, even when he's ravaging me. We *talk* now, too, which was something we staunchly avoided in the past. I have to say, I'm enjoying learning about Ransom Scott, and I think he's enjoying learning about me. I don't care to know the why of it. I just want to soak it up while I can. I'm living minute to minute, in case the dream ends.

It's Saturday and instead of meeting my friends for drinks, we're watching a program about the history of the cosmos, lying in each other's arms. This is the best kind of day—laying around, doing absolutely nothing but enjoying being in each other's company. Ransom has been quiet all afternoon, another thing he does from time to time. When he's quiet like this, I know he has something on his mind.

My thumbs trace over his strong forearms that are wrapped securely around my waist, following the map of thick veins as I watch stars collide on screen. I swear these programs could make a person go insane. Everything is a doomsday scenario. But I'm more concerned with whatever is going on in Ransom's head than my possibly imminent death.

"You're thinking pretty hard there, champ," I say to distract myself from the morbid thoughts circling in my brain. "Feel like sharing?"

His chest rises up and falls back down heavily, and he gives me a little squeeze. "I was just wondering what you might say if I invited you to come to dinner with me at my parents' house next week."

I twist in his arms to look at him. "I thought we were keeping us quiet for now."

His dark eyes pool with confliction. "I know, but we won't be on campus. Technically, we wouldn't even be going out in public."

"But a dinner with your parents? Why now? Why not wait until, I don't know *after* I graduate?" *When it's safe*, I add mentally. When I'm not just the student trying to earn an easy *A* by sleeping with her professor.

Slipping out from behind me, I roll onto my back as he positions himself above me. I wrap my legs around his hips and stare up at him, momentarily stunned by his beauty. Ransom's long, dark lashes are enviable, as are his flawless skin and perfect mouth. I still can't believe I've caught the attention of a man like him.

Brushing my hair behind my ears, he says, "My parents don't have to know the circumstance of our relationship. They just want to meet you."

"Oh, my God, you told them about us?" I'm floored and a little horrified. I only just told Annie, and the only reason for that was because she caught us red-handed. If she hadn't been standing on the other side of the door that morning, she would still be operating under the assumption that I wanted nothing more to do with him.

"Only that I had met someone. My brother is coming to town next week, and they're having a little dinner for him. They want me to bring you along."

An introduction and a welcome home dinner—this doesn't sound like just a casual thing. This sounds more like a big deal to me. But then I look at Ransom, and it's all over. His smile is soft and pleading, kryptonite to a hopeless romantic like me.

My brows scrunch together. "Stop looking at me like that. You know I can't say no to you when you look like a whipped puppy."

"Is that a yes?"

I take in his wide, knowing smile and shrug because there's no sense in trying to deny him. Not when he looks so adorable. "You know it is."

Rocking his pelvis against mine, he reawakens the passion I thought we'd knocked out earlier that morning. I tighten my legs around his hips, pulling him even closer, and he presses down into me, his arousal evident through his jeans. "They're going to love you."

"Well, they'd better," I say lightly, "because I'm awesome."

His chest rumbles with laughter. "Damn right you are."

I tilt my head, my lips pursing as something occurs to me. "Does this mean I'm your girlfriend?"

Leaning down, Ransom kisses me softly. "Do you want to be?"

"I think I do," I say, lifting up to run my tongue along his jaw.

He groans, moving his head to the side as I continue on down his neck. "Then it's settled. Now put your hand down my pants and play with my cock."

"I'm not even your girlfriend for two minutes and already you're demanding things of me," I tease as I release the button on his jeans. "I hope you don't think this means you own me."

"Oh, baby," he growls as I take him into my hand. "I've owned you since the moment I laid eyes on you. You just didn't know it."

***

As far as being Ransom's girlfriend goes, it's pretty unremarkable. In fact, it's just what I imagine being in a relationship with a regular guy my age would be, just with a dash of cloak and dagger crap. Dating on the DL means we can't be seen together outside of class, and if we cross paths in public, it's a simple, quick *hello* and we're on our way. Going into it, I hadn't realized how hard it would be to actually be with him, but it is. It so is.

After spending the rest of the day together, Ransom suggested that I get out of the house and reconnect with the outside world. He was right, of course. As much as I would like to dominate all of his time, it's not healthy to be so wrapped up in another person. Plus, his isn't the only relationship I need to nurture, and I assume the same is true for him. So, we agreed to part ways for the weekend. I spent most of mine at home catching up on homework and wondering what Ransom was up to. Was he working, too? Visiting family? Or catching up with someone else—Red perhaps? Even now, the thought makes my stomach knot up. He hadn't exactly been shy about shoving her under my nose before. What was to say he wouldn't continue seeing her behind my back?

Already, trust is a major factor.

Another thing that's not normal about us: I don't have any way to contact him. No number. No address. Outside of the classroom, I have no earthly clue how to get in touch with him.

"Are you kidding me?" Annie looks appalled. I don't know why I told her any of this, but sharing the load makes it somewhat more bearable. "What kind of relationship is this anyway?"

"A secret one," I whisper harshly over the table. Maybe discussing this over lunch in the cafeteria first thing on a Monday wasn't such a good idea. There are students everywhere.

Leaning over her steaming cup of vanilla chai tea, she says, "It sounds more like a booty call. You can't seriously tell me that you're okay with this."

No, I can't. I thought I was okay with it, but I'm beginning to realize this is just another phase of our hotel room arrangement. Only now, he gets to save himself the added cost of screwing me.

I think of how Ransom looked at me this morning in class. Nothing that would be obvious to an outsider, but I recognized that look in his eye, the subtle, secret smile recalling memories that only he and I share. It almost wiped away the worries that have been worming their way into my psyche.

God, I'm an idiot.

Poking at my tuna salad, I can't meet her eyes. I feel defensive, like she's attacking me, even though she hasn't said one word against me. "You don't know him. He's sweet."

"Sweet? He's *sweet*? Honey, seriously, pull your head out of the sand. This may have been cute before, but it's not now. He's just another man abusing his power. Instead of turning a blind eye, you need to be asking yourself how many other girls he's done this with."

My gaze snaps up, and my mouth curves down. I could hurl the same words back at her about her relationship, but I leave the dying argument lying on the table between us. There's no sense in getting into a fight over something that I know Ransom wouldn't do. But even as I think it, I question how certain I really am.

Despite where we started, as far as I know, Ransom's one of the good guys. He's been upfront about everything right from the start. There's no reason to search for deception. But who's to say that there isn't a trail of teary-eyed girls laid out behind me? What if I'm not the exception to the rule? The thought is unsettling and I move to change the topic.

"How are you and Jason doing?"

Annie sits up straight in her chair, flips her blonde hair over her shoulder, and focused on her tea as if she's hoping to see her future in it. "Good. Some things came up and we talked. I think we're in a good place right now."

Something in her voice catches my attention. It tells me to follow up, and I do. "*Some things?* What does that mean?"

I don't miss the way her gaze skitters around the room, nor the way she chews her bottom lip like it's candy. When she finally looks at me, she's wearing this strange expression that makes me nervous. "Jason accepted a job in California…and he asked me to go with him."

I can't breathe. It feels like someone sucked all the oxygen out of the room and my lungs are about to collapse. I flounder for something to say, but all I come up with is an angry, "Are you crazy!"

Annie doesn't appear the least bit surprised by my outburst, although a couple heads turn to see what the fuss is about. "I've thought about it a lot over the last week, and I believe that this is a good move."

"You *think*?" I huff. Unbelievable. The one person in my life, who I thought had a good head on her shoulders, has lost her ever-loving mind. I may not know a ton about Jason, but what I do know is enough for me to say that she's too good for him and she'll regret it. "To move halfway across the country, you'd better be a hell of a lot more positive than that."

I'm mad. Steaming. Ready to hunt down Jason and kick him in the sack for trying to take my friend away.

"I am sure, Joe." She sighs, reaching across the table and placing her hand over mine. I think about pulling it away, but I don't. I leave it there and decide to hear her out. "This isn't a snap decision. There's more to it than just deciding to follow my boyfriend to Cali."

"Then why don't you tell me, because right now, I'm seriously upset with you. I can't believe that you'd just up and leave me alone like this. Sisters before misters, remember?"

"You know Jason and I had a plan." She slowly draws back and I can tell that whatever she wants to say, she's afraid. Why would she be afraid to talk to me?

Realization hits me and I slump back in my chair. Why else would a woman walk away from her life, unless she was given a very good reason? "Oh, my God. You're pregnant."

Her emerald eyes flare and her mouth drops open for a split second, before setting into a firm line. I have my answer. Stunned, frustrated, worried…so many emotions run through me that I can't get a handle on them all.

Sliding my chair back, I dump my tray in the garbage and stride toward the exit. Annie calls after me, but it's just background noise.

Seventeen

I sing, badly. But that doesn't stop me from trying. The next song is "Dance Magic" and I roll right into it, even though I hate David Bowie. I'm much more of a Billy Idol kind of girl.

There is no shame in admitting that you are alone and plastered before dinner time on a Monday, especially if there is no one you know around to see you crashing and burning in a puddle of self-pity.

Why a puddle of self-pity? I'm still trying to figure that out. I just know that there is this ache in my chest that is only dulled by the burn of alcohol, so I keep pouring more, hoping to lose myself so completely that this day will be nothing more than a black hole in my memory. But, after I lose my balance and nearly break my ankle, I do the smartest thing I've done all day—I throw in the towel and drop down on the couch.

The silence that follows drives home how alone I truly am, and when I kill the music, the lively atmosphere in the living room dies along with it.

Life sucks. Anyone who says differently is a liar or an idiot. Taking on the responsibilities of an adult before you know how to be one sucks. Losing both parents before the age of eighteen sucks. Using your body to get by might sound like a fantasy to some, but in reality, it sucks. Knowing you have very little claim on the man you call your boyfriend sucks, too.

From the very first breath we take, we're destined to experience pain. I've experienced enough of it that it's begun to drown out any happiness that might dare come my way. Some days, my senses feel dulled, my emotions diluted. I ignore it all and push on. Otherwise nothing would get done. All of it, every last bit, just plain sucks.

I lift my half-empty glass of scotch and toast the air, then slug it down. The burn feels good, makes me feel alive. Then the lethargy begins to kick in, and I figure, why not have another? Maybe this one will do the trick. There's no one here to tell me to stop, no one here to judge my actions. It's just me and the bottle.

I pour myself another glass. And another. I don't remember crawling into bed, but I do remember waking up in the middle of the night. Just snippets of memory really. The room spinning, my stomach pitching and rolling with it. An unseen hand holding my hair back as I retch into a bucket beside the bed.

When I wake up in the morning, the sheets cling to me. The chill in the room causes goosebumps to erupt on my skin, but I'm sweating, as though I have a fever. The sun spilling through the partially opened curtains blinds me and my head pounds violently.

The humming in my ears is almost as bad—sharp and stabbing, like someone left a power drill running in my skull.

But wait.

I force myself to sit up and my body sways with the effort.

The drill isn't in my head, but somewhere else in the apartment. As I try to assess where exactly it's coming from, it stops. Moments tick by and I watch the doorway. One thought repeats in my head as I wait: A hand held my hair back.

Someone is in my apartment.

Quickly, I sift through my memory, compiling a list of who has a key to my place, but it's like wading through quicksand. My thoughts are sluggish, and by the time I think I've counted everyone, which is practically no one, as Annie and my landlord are the only two people who should have one, it's too late.

Ransom fills the doorway. He pauses when he sees me, a soft smile in his eyes. "You're awake. How are you feeling?"

I'm lost for words. I watch him stride into the room, his long legs eating up the carpet so fast my eyes strain to keep up, but I do. Dressed in only a pair of loose fitting jeans that hang low on his hips, revealing a sculpted torso, he's impossible to look away from. Makes it impossible to think.

A tall glass of green liquid is pushed in front of my face. "What's this?" I croak as I cautiously accept the offering. My nose scrunches up as I take a sniff. There is a medley of scents, all of which make me queasy.

"It's my mother's hangover remedy. It's guaranteed to clear your head and get you back on your feet."

By throwing up, I presume. "What's in it?"

"Just a few greens, some protein, and a couple vitamins. Drink."

His fingertips nudge the bottom of the glass, urging me to do as he says. I take a cautious sip. It's a balance between sweet and bitter, not altogether appalling. The grainy texture turns me off a bit, though, as does the slight smell of peanut butter, but I continue drinking until the cup is half gone and my stomach threatens to revolt.

Handing the glass over, I lie back down and close my eyes. Listening as Ransom sets the glass down and lowers himself onto the bed beside me, I'm reminded of a question I needed to ask.

"How did you get into my apartment?" I'd been in such a foul mood after leaving Annie, I hoped like hell my anger hadn't made me forget to lock up.

"I borrowed a spare I found in your junk drawer."

Somehow, that strikes me as even worse than forgetting to flip the locks. "So you just took it?"

"In case of an emergency."

I repeat his words to myself. For some reason, it strikes me as funny. Here's this man who I've been having sex with for months, who never cared a lick about my personal *anything* before, and suddenly, he's concerned about my welfare. "Why didn't you just ask?"

"Would you have given it to me if I had?"

I open my eyes and fall straight into his. They're blank, unreadable...and I don't know what I would have done. "I guess we'll never know."

He sighs. "No, I suppose we never will." Standing, he crosses to the door and bends down to scoop up a bundle of fresh sheets. "Go grab a shower. I'll take care of things in here."

I don't argue because as disgusting as I feel, I need a moment alone more.

I take my time showering and exploring how I feel about Ransom having a key to my place. I didn't give it to him, he took it. I'm not sure how I feel about that.

On one hand, I'm ticked off that he had the audacity to just help himself. It's basically stealing, but should I really be surprised? I've never known him to be courteous or particularly concerned with other people's feelings.

On the other hand, I'm happy he's here. I don't know what possessed him to let himself inside—a surprise visit?—but I know that he helped me last night when he didn't have to.

By the time I turn off the water, I've decided to let Ransom slide on a technicality. As embarrassed as I am that he saw me at my worst—*for the second time*—he took care of me. He stayed and made sure I was okay, and he's still here.

I find Ransom braced against the countertop, waiting for me. His features grow darker as I step out of the shower and wrap myself in a towel. For a moment, we just stare at each other. I feel as though, despite the time we've spent together, there's something I'm missing. Something I'm overlooking, but for the life of me, I can't put my finger on it. It's not the first time I've felt this way, and it's disconcerting.

"Are you mad that I have a key?" His voice is a low rumble and I detect a hint of concern.

"No, just surprised." Reaching around him, I retrieve a comb and lead us into the kitchen where I begin working the tangles from my hair while a pot of coffee brews.

There's only one question still nagging at me, and I ask it again, even though I suspect I already know what his answer will be. "Why didn't you ask?"

Ransom's mouth twists and he repeats his earlier question. "Would you have given it to me?"

I already know my answer, but I take a moment to think it over anyway. When it doesn't change, I tell him, "No, probably not."

He gives me a look that says *that's why*. I have to grit my teeth to keep from saying something I'll regret.

"Why did you come over last night? I thought we were spending some time apart."

Ransom moves behind the counter that overlooks the living room and pours a cup of coffee. He drinks it black. "Do I need a reason?"

"No." I shake my head. Something tells me to tread lightly. The way Ransom's shoulders seem to bunch up, and the tension he's throwing off, makes me uneasy. "How long are you staying?"

His eyes meet mine over the rim of his cup. "Is that a nice way of asking me to leave?"

"Again, no. Just making conversation over here. I think the question is perfectly reasonable." *Especially since I didn't invite you over in the first place.* I don't voice that to him though. I have the feeling he's spoiling for a fight, and I'm not going to give it to him. Not with the…Wait. What the hell happened to my hangover? With the amount of alcohol I put away last night, I should be laid out in bed right now.

"What did you put in that drink again?" I rub my temples, testing for aches and pains, but the only thing I detect is the slightest, almost insignificant strain behind my eyes.

Ransom smirks. "Told you it worked. Doesn't smell or taste the greatest, but it never fails to deliver." Abandoning his cup on the counter, he walks over and cups my face in his large palm. His thumb strokes over my jaw and presses into my chin as he tilts my head back.

"I'm glad you're feeling okay. With the state you were in last night, I wasn't sure you would be."

"Even with your magic potion?"

He smiles faintly at my attempt to lighten the mood. "Even with it, yes. That's the second time I've seen you like that. The first time I understand. You were having fun. But this time was different. You seemed…sad. Why is that?"

I get lost in his eyes so easily—dark eyes that see straight through me. When Ransom looks at me like this, I feel a pull to tell him everything, to confess all my secrets. It's the princess complex. The innate desire to have a man who cares enough to swoop in and solve all my problems. But that's the problem. Ransom isn't that man...Is he?

Months ago, I would have said no, he isn't, and been one-hundred percent certain I was right. Now, I don't know what to make of him.

"I got some news that I didn't like." I shrug and slip from his hold, eager to drop this conversation. It's too early to get too heavy.

Grabbing a fistful of his black AC/DC concert t-shirt now covering his gorgeous chest, I plaster myself against him. "I never thanked you for fixing me up. What do you say we head back to the bedroom so I can show you how grateful I am."

Ransom's smile is dark, dangerous, and oh so sexy. I have a hard time catching my breath as he sets his cup aside and backs me into the hallway. Little touches are how he teases me— sliding a finger across my cheek, tracing my bottom lip, skating a path from throat to sternum, creating an invisible line between my breasts. Once we're in my bedroom, he tugs my towel away.

Standing naked before Ransom has always been thrilling, if not a little terrifying. I anticipate the predatory gleam that he always gets in his eyes whenever we're about to have sex. It's how I know what kind of mood he's in. It's always been aggressive, but tonight, there's no sign of it. In its place, I only see desire. There's a feral heat lingering in their depths, but Ransom's eyes are gentle, almost placid.

Like he's seeing *me*.

I wonder what he sees. A woman who is confident in her own skin? Or a woman who has devalued herself by taking off her clothes for other men? That's my fear, the one that wiggles a little deeper into my gray matter every time I step onto that stage. What kind of guy would want a woman who strips for a living? Someone who shows off their body to anyone with a dollar to wave.

Sometimes, I don't even like myself, so how can *he* like me?

Ransom strips off his clothes, dropping them on the floor where they join mine, and we are both standing naked before one another. His body is one that makes every muscle inside of me clench. One look and I burn for his touch. I shiver when he circles his arms around me and guides us to the bed. I stretch out beneath him, and as I look into his eyes I catch a glimpse of something that gives me pause.

For the briefest moment, it makes sense. It's not what he sees in me that keeps him coming back. It's what I see in him. He looks at me with wonderment. With a vulnerability that suggests being with me gives him something he needs.

Suddenly, I don't see the same man who throws me against doors and drives into me with little care beyond his own desires. I see a man who needs to be cared for. A man who just might be as lost as I have been since the day I lost my mother. Without a second thought, I open my arms to that man and accept him inside of me, and together we lose ourselves in the temporary pleasure of each other's body.

Eighteen

Annie's driving me crazy. I can't escape the guilt of walking away from her. I'm sitting in the back of the room of Art Comp, trying to concentrate on taking notes, but it's impossible when she keeps finding any excuse she can to look back at me.

After she had texted me a dozen times last week, I broke down and told Ransom what happened. He thinks I need to get over it and apologize. I know he's right. I know I'm being petty, but this feels like a betrayal. Annie's my only real friend and while I always knew our lives would lead us down different paths after college, I always thought we'd remain close.

I never thought our lives would end up thousands of miles apart.

I'm not stupid. I know once she's gone, we'll never see each other again. All the promises in the world won't make a difference once she's out in California starting the next chapter of her life. She's going to be a mother—I still can't wrap my head around that one—which leaves no room for me. At best, we might exchange an occasional email or phone call, but it won't be the same. *We* won't be the same.

I'm wasting time being angry with her, but I don't know how else to deal with everything I'm feeling inside of me. So, for now, I'm keeping my distance.

When class lets out, I gather my books and hope that I'll get lost in the wave of students leaving the room, but Annie is waiting for me at the bottom of the stairs when I get there. I'm not ready to talk to her yet.

As I reach the last step, an uncertain smile grows on her face, and a low hum starts up inside my head. "Can we talk for a minute?"

Annie wears her emotions on her sleeve, so it's not hard to tell that she is hurt by my behavior. Still, as much as I want to reach out and pull her in for a hug and assure her it's going to be fine, I don't. The excuse falls from my lips before I know it's coming.

"I can't. I have to talk with Professor Scott about the final project."

Her eyes are locked with mine, searching, and I know she can tell I'm lying, but she lets it slide. "Okay, well, maybe we can catch up later then."

I smile tightly, because we both know it's unlikely. But it's nice to pretend. "Sure."

Annie doesn't leave right away, making it impossible to keep up my ruse. If I linger, the lie will be exposed. Maybe that's what's she's going for. Maybe she's trying to beat me at my own game. I catch her giving me a sidelong look as she stacks her papers neatly into her backpack, and that's all the confirmation I need. The little devil is cleverer than I thought.

Realizing I have to follow through with my bogus excuse, I slowly walk toward Ransom's desk, where he is seated, his head down, as he quietly flips through an overlarge art book.

I clear my throat to get him to notice me, and when he lifts his head, his smile is bright. Too bright. I dart my eyes over my shoulder and he follows the movement, seeing Annie. His smile instantly turns professional.

"What can I do for you, Miss Hart?"

I hadn't intended to tell him. My plan was to wait until the last possible moment and then slap my name at the bottom of the project list, but Annie has put me in a tight position and I can't think of anything else right now.

Drawing in a deep breath, I say in a rush, "I signed up to pose for Mrs. Jackson's modeling class for the final project."

Ransom's expression flattens out, so I can't tell what he's thinking. From the corner of my eye, I see Annie paused just outside the door, and when I glance up at her, she grins and shoots me a thumb up. I can't help smiling back. She's the one who pushed me to do this. Even though I'm mad at her, it feels good to share my secret with her and to know that she supports me.

When she's gone, I refocus my attention on Ransom, who is studiously avoiding my gaze. "I thought your friend was going to do that."

"She was, but she changed her mind. Since her spot was open, and I hadn't settled on anything, I decided to fill it."

Leaning back in his chair, Ransom stares me down as his thumb repeatedly clicks the pen in his hand. The longer he does it, the more I feel the tension between us grow. He's upset. It doesn't take a rocket scientist to deduce that.

"Why would you choose to take off your clothes for a roomful of people?"

I freeze because he's got to be kidding. Out of everyone on campus, why wouldn't I do it? It's right up my alley. Some might even say that it's a natural progression. From partially nude to fully naked.

"I'm not ashamed of my body," I tell him. "Plus, it's a paying gig."

"So you're doing it for the money?"

"Every college student needs extra money wherever they can get it, right?" The fire snapping in his eyes tells me he doesn't agree.

"If you needed money, you should have asked me. You don't have to subject yourself to a bunch of horny frat boys to get it."

I laugh. "Do you really think *frat boys* would take an art class just to see a naked chick? All they have to do is snap a finger and girls everywhere will drop their clothes at their feet."

"I think you're missing the point here."

"What, that you don't agree with my choice? I disagree," I reply smartly. "I think the message was pretty clear."

His dark eyes narrow at my tone and I glare right back. As his next class begins to file in, I toss back my hair and adopt a carefree attitude. "Can I borrow your pen for a minute? I'd like to add my name before I forget."

After writing my name down, I return the pen to his desk. Ransom doesn't say another word as I leave the room.

I'm not the least bit surprised to see him lurking in the shadows when I walk onto the stage later that night.

My stomach flutters in nervous anticipation as my song ends and I step off the stage. I half expect him to barge into the dressing room like he did last time, but he doesn't do that either. By the time I'm through freshening up and head back out onto the floor to begin serving drinks, I'm confident that I've figured out his game.

He's going to make me sweat.

Ransom's a master at playing head games. He likes to watch and wait. Make a girl shake before he goes in for the kill. I love and hate this game. It's a constant adrenalin rush that's hard to come down from. My hands tremble as I carry an order of drinks to a table positioned only a few feet from his.

Once again, he's cloaked in shadows. I used to wonder why he did that. Now I assume it must be because he worries he'll be recognized. A professor in a strip club probably isn't the best image to put out there.

I feel his eyes on me as I slide the drinks in front of my customers. Two men, middle-aged, with touches of gray in their hair. They're dressed in paint-splattered navy overalls, suggesting they came directly after work. A lot of men do that. They come for a few drinks and a good show to help them unwind.

"How are you fellas enjoying your evening?" Gripping the back of one of the chairs, I lean into one hip. The position pushes my butt out, creating a nice S-curve in my back. Ransom loves that. What he doesn't love, though, is another man's hands on his property.

I learn this lesson pretty quick when the man whose chair I am holding winds his arm around my waist and plants a firm hand on my right butt cheek.

His coffee-stained smile is gone in an instant and so is mine as I am jerked backward and Ransom steps in to take my place.

I would have fallen on my ass had he not reacted so quickly and grabbed ahold of my arm at the last second. Turning ferocious eyes gone black on the man, who now wears a look that is a cross between surprised, pissed off, and a touch frightened, Ransom growls a warning that makes even me shiver.

"If you *ever* touch her again, I'll rip that filthy hand off and shove it so far up your ass you'll spend the rest of your life wiping it with a stump. Are we clear?"

The man nods, his wide eyes unblinking. Ransom holds his gaze for a few beats more, and then he turns on me. With his hand still firmly wrapped around my arm, he hustles me away. The bathrooms are just beyond the bar, and I muster a half-hearted smile so Bernice doesn't sick security on us.

Fear is a very real factor here as I am bundled into the men's bathroom. An older man stands in front of the sinks, washing his hands, and when Ransom aims his death glare on him and tells him to hit the road, he doesn't waste a second thinking about it.

Once we're alone, I am crowded against the wall. Ransom's tall, solid frame is heavy and borderline oppressive. But when he gathers my hands over my head and begins tearing at my skirt until it is gathered around my waist, my labored breaths are no longer a result of fear.

"Are you mad at me?" I gasp as his fingers find my hot center and plunge inside, working my internal temperature up so high I feel as though I could combust.

Burying his face in the curve between my neck and shoulder, he rasps against my skin, "I'm mad at that fucker for putting his hands on what's mine."

That doesn't really answer my question, but I figure it's probably the only one I'm going to get. His teeth scrape down my throat and he licks my collarbone as he works his way lower to the swell of my breasts. It's difficult to think when he's kissing me like this.

"My boss isn't going to be happy if he hears you chased off one of his customers. You know, we have security for that sort of thing."

Releasing a low, frustrated growl, Ransom tears the flimsy hunter green thong from my body as if it's made of paper, and insinuates himself between my thighs. The move places the hardest part of him right against my core. I moan from the contact.

"Fuck security. They're slow and lazy."

"They're effective when they need to be."

"I just pulled one of their workers off the floor and forced her into the bathroom after threatening a patron. Listen." He pauses, tilting his head. His eyes have a dangerous gleam in them when he looks back at me. "I don't hear the pitter patter of little feet coming to the rescue, do you?"

I roll my eyes. "That's because I told Bernice I was fine."

"I didn't hear you say a word."

I smirk. "Haven't you heard? Women don't need words to communicate effectively."

"The only woman I grew up with was my mom. Guess I didn't learn that skill."

I love the smile that blooms on his face. It's cute and teasing and it sets off little creases around his eyes that remind me of his more playful, easygoing side. I like this side, too, though, and right now, it has my hormones raging.

I moan into his mouth as he kisses me, his tongue plunging past my lips to slide over mine. Releasing my hands, Ransom grabs the backs of my thighs and hoists me up. Like a perfectly choreographed dance, I wrap my legs around his lean hips and tunnel my fingers into his hair, pulling him so I can taste his mouth as he burrows a hand between our bodies and unzips his fly.

His hard length nudges my opening and our kiss becomes more aggressive. I'm panting for oxygen when he tears his mouth from mine. I whimper, needing more of him, but he stops everything.

When I realize that he's not going any further, I peel my eyes open to find him staring at me with intense concentration.

"No one touches you but me."

My brows pull down at the sudden change I'm witnessing in him. "Okay," I say, stretching the word out.

"I mean it. You're mine. What happened out there? You make sure that never happens again."

A part of me perks up, irritated that he thinks he can tell me what to do. "Do you realize who you're talking to? I'm a stripper. It happens."

He shakes his head slowly. "You're not getting it. I don't care who you are or what you do, that doesn't happen again. I don't share, understand? You're mine, and as mine, the only hands that touch this ass belong to me."

I don't know whether to be upset or overjoyed at his caveman behavior. "Are you claiming me?"

"Honey, I claimed you the first time I saw you dance on that stage." His mouth crashes over mine. Our teeth bang together from the force of our passion. With one brutal thrust of his hips, Ransom is inside of me. I cry out as my body instantly releases, my muscles milking him with such force that Ransom follows right behind me.

Our mingled breaths echo in the room as we float back down to earth. His heartbeat drums against my chest, and I hold him tighter to my breasts. There's nothing better than post-coital Ransom. For a few, brief moments, he's completely mine. It's in these moments, when he's at his softest that a woman could lose her way.

But Ransom puts an end to those troubling thoughts when he pulls back and sets me on my feet. I am a mess. My clothes are bunched around my waist, my underwear hanging in useless strings, and his cum is leaking down my thighs. He didn't use a condom this time, and I thank whoever is listening above that I had enough sense to get on birth control. When I look at myself in the mirror, there is cherry red lipstick smeared across my face, which is the icing to my disheveled state.

The same goes for Ransom, but even rumpled and stained crimson, he is completely edible.

"You know, as much as I enjoy these little rendezvous, we really must stop meeting up like this," I say as I begin cleaning myself up.

After zipping himself back up, Ransom positions himself beside the sink, lifting one arm in the air to press against the wall. With his suit jacket hanging open to expose the white shirt beneath and the expensive silver buckle on the black leather belt circling his narrow waist, he looks like he belongs on the cover of GQ.

"What do you mean?"

"I say, for public decency's sake, we should probably keep our activities confined to a bed. Yours perhaps? I've never seen your apartment."

Instantly, he throws up an invisible wall and I know I've said the wrong thing, pushed him too hard. "And you won't."

His harsh tone confounds me and I watch in disbelief as he straightens. Refusing to look at me as he fastens the single button on his jacket and walks toward the door.

"You'll forgive me," he says firmly, "but I have business to attend to."

My mouth gapes open, but no words come out. After what we just did, I thought we were in a good place.

When am I going to learn that sex isn't a magic fix? It doesn't mend relationships. Rather, it's like plugging a hole in a sinking ship with caulk—utterly ineffective. As soon as you stop filling the hole, it begins leaking again.

Once I put myself back together again enough to return to the floor, I don't bother looking around for him. Ransom is long gone and I'm not in the mood to chase after him. Maybe it's for the best. Maybe this is the wake-up call I need to realize that it's time to let go of something that was never going to be.

Nineteen

I can't get the strange look Ransom shot me, when I declined his invitation to meet him after class, out of my head. It's almost as if he didn't understand why I might be upset with him. At the very least, he should recognize that walking away from a woman in the middle of a discussion, directly following hot and heavy sex, is definite grounds for a problem. That he doesn't shouldn't be a surprise to me, but it is. I was just starting to get used to New Ransom, and then Old, Callous Ransom reared his head again.

Worst of all, I like both sides of him. I like his overbearing, bullheaded, take-charge attitude just as much as I like the more subdued, almost domestic side of his personality.

That's where I made my first mistake. I allowed myself to get comfortable and forget who he really was. *What* this really is. Sex. Nothing more than good, casual sex. What happened in the bathroom is the perfect example of what we are. It would be prudent of me to not forget that again.

Over the course of the last week, I have lost my best friend and the boyfriend I thought I had. My world feels like it's imploding. A smart person would point out that I am clearly the problem in at least one of those equations and it's fully within my power to fix it.

I am not a smart person. Clearly. Otherwise, I wouldn't be standing in the middle of a crowded bar on a Friday night ordering another pitcher for the table I am sharing with a guy who I know has feelings for me—the kind I don't return.

My life is like a train speeding down unfinished tracks. One of these days, it will hit the end and plunge into the abyss. I need to stomp on the brakes now, but my common sense has fallen asleep at the wheel.

Brody jumps out of his seat as I walk up with my hands full and takes the pitchers. "I brought two," I state the obvious as I drop into the hardwood chair.

"So we won't run out." Brody taps his temple. "Excellent thinking, J."

I mock bow. Well, as much as I can given my seated position. "As always, I aim to please."

Brody's eyes flicker with appreciation as he scans my appearance. "Have I told you how good you look tonight?"

Topping off my glass, I respond coyly. "Only twenty times or so, but hearing it never gets old. You may refresh my memory."

"You look really good tonight."

I wink at him, and instantly regret it. I'm leading Brody on, giving him false hope. There must be something wrong with me because I can't seem to help myself. I'm a shameless flirt. Maybe that's why Ransom warned me against other men, because he knows it's as much my fault as it is theirs?

"Hey," Brody shouts over the loud pop country music. "You're thinking too hard and it's sucking all the fun from the room."

Standing, he reaches for my hand. I'm given no time to prepare an argument as he whisks me onto the dance floor.

"I don't know this song," I shout. I feel like I've just entered a *Footloose* audition and forgot to study. Everyone, and I mean everyone, seems to have attended some dance class I wasn't privy to. They're all partnered up, performing the same moves at the same time.

Brody pulls me against his chest, his eyes glued to what's happening around us. "You don't have to know it," he replies distractedly. "You just have to have fun."

A startled scream bursts past my lips and I suddenly find myself being spun around and around the dance floor, weaving in and out of other couples' paths.

And then the most wonderful thing happens.

I'm laughing. I don't know when I started, but I'm having fun, and when I look around, everyone else is, too. Brody's smile is wider than I've ever seen it. Clasping my hand, he holds it against his chest, and my grip on his shoulder tightens as we pick up the pace to match the beat of the music.

"Where did you learn to dance like this?" I'm winded, but the feeling of my heart beating so fast is exhilarating.

"About five minutes ago!"

I don't believe him, because he's *that* good, but as I watch him studying everyone around us, I realize he's serious. "Are you telling me you just watched everyone dancing and jumped in?"

"Yep." His grin is infectious.

I shake my head. "You're crazy!"

The music cuts off at the exact moment the words leave my lips, and my voice is broadcast to the whole bar. My face heats and I bite my lip.

Brody's shoulders shake with laughter. It's then I realize that I'm still holding onto him. With a nervous smile, I drop my hands and sever all contact.

Placing his hand on my lower back, Brody walks us back to our table. Just before we reach it, he leans down, placing his lips against the shell of my ear. "You're right, I am crazy. *For you*."

My jaw drops and my head jerks up. I'm prepared to tell him all the reasons why he shouldn't like me, why we'll only ever work as friends, but the words are literally stolen away.

Brody's lips land firmly on mine. He doesn't ask my permission. Doesn't waste time coaxing me to kiss him back. He just takes. Devours. Unbidden, my body sways toward his, and I fall deeper into the kiss.

And just like that, I've managed to find myself in a love triangle.

My head is filled with static, as if a bomb just went off, and as my hearing slowly returns, so too does my reasoning. When I realize what I am doing, I break our lip lock so fast Brody has to grip the table to keep from losing his balance.

I know I must look like a girl who just realized her boyfriend is an axe murderer, because Brody's face morphs from utter bliss to a mask of concern in the split second it takes for me to throw my purse over my shoulder.

"I have to go," I tell him wildly. "I'm so sorry, but this was a mistake. I have to go."

I turn to run, but it feels as though I've stepped into quicksand. Time slows to a halt and the buzzing in my ears returns en force. Standing less than a few feet away is Ransom. His face is completely void of all emotion, and the lack thereof is so much worse than if he'd yelled. I feel like a fist is in my chest squeezing my heart.

I gasp, but that's all the sound I get out. I've reached the end of the track, and my train is tumbling over the edge right before my eyes.

Unable to watch the wreckage unfold, I force my leaden legs to move and before I know it, I am running out the door, running from Brody, from Ransom. From everything.

I don't look back.

***

Brody catches up with me on the side of the road, and I am too ashamed to explain to him everything that's going on in my head. Thankfully, he doesn't force it. Like the gentleman that he is, he takes me home and when I tell him good-night, he leaves it at that.

I don't get so lucky with Ransom. He shows up soon after Brody leaves, banging down the door because his key can't get past the chain. I ignore him until one of the neighbors threatens to call the cops.

Forced to let him in or see him arrested for disturbing the peace, which will no doubt lead to a whole new set of problems, I sit through his long, impassioned speech over how hurt he was to see me kiss another man, which seems so unlike him, until he begins questioning my morals, my integrity. He asks me about my feelings for him, about what I want out of all of this, but my answer keeps coming back the same—I don't know.

What am I supposed to say? It's the truth. I have no idea where I stand with him anymore. I've never had to give it much thought. Being with Ransom was supposed to be easy, no strings. Hell, we were never even supposed to know each other's names. Instead, it has left me so knotted up inside, I don't know whether I like him, love him or am simply in love with the idea of him. My entire life has been tossed into the air, and all I keep seeing is big, fat question marks stamped on everything as it falls back down around my feet.

Ransom drops to his knees before me with a tortured look on his face. I instantly recoil inside, because that look comes with expectations that I can't handle right now. I have to figure out how to handle *me* first.

"Out of everyone, I never would have expected you to be capable of doing that, but I'm also man enough to accept some of the blame."

I am surprised by this. Ransom is a lot of things, but I never would have expected him to admit such a fault. "I'm the one who kissed another man."

"You wouldn't have done it if I hadn't given you reason to," he contends. "I've been giving you mixed messages, I know that. The truth is, we never should have hooked up, and it's not fair for me to ask you to hide us from everyone." Stricken, he reaches out, his fingers touching my face. "Tell me to leave, and I will. If it makes things better for you, I'll walk away right now, Josephine."

Do I want him to go away? I try to picture never feeling his skin on mine again, never hearing his roughened voice in my ear after we've had sex, never knowing the look of true passion that I see in his eyes every time he looks at me.

My throat tightens and I shake my head. "I don't want you to go." The truth is there are a lot of things I would change between us. I would start with throwing out all this secrecy and telling everyone about us. I could do with a little less of the split personalities, too, but Rome wasn't built in a day.

"But you don't want me to stay, either." It's a statement, and I can't help wondering what he saw in my face to make him reach that conclusion.

My lungs fill until my chest feels tight, and I release my breath on a heavy sigh. "I want things to change."

His expression tightens and his hand falls away, leaving my cheek cold. "I can't go public."

"I know." I sigh again. I don't know whether it was the alcohol or the fact that I've been up for over twelve hours straight, but I feel drained. My whole life has been one secret—from the stripping to him and other things that I can't bring myself to think about—and I'm exhausted.

I continue, and though it breaks my heart, the words have to be said. "That's the problem, Ransom. You can't tell anyone, but I can't continue to keep up this secrecy. It's too much maintenance and it's wearing thin. *I'm* wearing thin."

"So that's it? We're done?" He's upset, and I understand that, but I have to think of myself first. I've made a lot of sacrifices in my lifetime, and it's time I take something back. I'm starting with my life. I won't be held prisoner by someone who doesn't think as highly of me as I do them.

"I need to be with someone who wants to tell the world about me," I explain, hoping to smooth away some of the sting. "Not someone who is ashamed to be seen with me."

"I'm not ashamed of you," Ransom says through clenched teeth.

I tilt my head, my smile small and sad. "We have sex, Ransom. That's all we do. We've never been out on a date, never kissed in public, never taken a drive together. None of the things real couples do."

"We drove together once."

"Three times and they don't count," I say, thinking of the time his car broke down and I dropped him at the hotel and other times when I was drunk. If I recall correctly, that first time he was meeting a "friend." Most likely the same friend who showed up with him hours later at the club for a private dance. I admit, it's something that still bothers me if I think on it too long.

"Your friend knows about me. My parents know about you. I asked you to come to dinner with me." His silky voice has taken on a pleading tone, a last ditch effort to sway my decision, but it's already been made.

I shake my head. Standing, I slip past him and walk to the front door. Opening it, I stand in the doorway and pass him a meaningful look. "I'm sorry, but it's just not enough."

He has this hateful look in his eyes, but it's not directed at me. I think he hates himself, or maybe the situation. I know how he feels. I never wanted things to end between us, but here we are, standing in my doorway, and it's over. Saying goodbye is a physical ache in my chest, but it has to be done. I see no other way.

Ransom stands over me, and it's all I can do not to fall into his arms and take back everything I just said. "You know I wish things had been different."

"So do I." But they aren't. He's still my professor, and I'm still his student, and let's face it, this relationship has never been healthy.

He nods, his gaze shifting from the hall to my face like he's not sure he can take that first step. Then, without any warning, I'm in his arms and his mouth is on mine and I am breathing and tasting him and all of my senses are exploding because this man—*this man*—is the one I want. Have always wanted. And he isn't mine. Can't be mine.

He lets me go as fast as he took me, and then he's gone. I watch him walk out my door and out of my life and I don't know whether to be relieved or just very, very sad.

Twenty

Being alone isn't my strong suit. I've always made sure that someone is there to keep me from losing myself in my thoughts. It's not a design that I follow on purpose, but more of a survival instinct. I need someone there to catch me if I fall. That's why I finally decided to pull up my big girl panties and return Annie's calls.

She's surprised to hear from me. Of course, she is. I've been blowing her off ever since she told me she was moving out of state. If she knew why I was calling her now, she'd probably tell me to take a long jump off a short bridge. A certain amount of guilt comes with that. Knowing that I am essentially using her to keep me from doing something even more stupid, like asking Ransom to take me back.

We're curled up on the country blue sofa in Annie's living room facing each other. She's wearing a soft white, fuzzy sweater that looks like someone skinned Sasquatch and black skinny jeans, and she's glowing.

"I'm really happy you're here," she says for the tenth time since I walked through the door.

"Me, too," I say honestly. I've never felt more at home than I have with this girl. She's my soft place.

Her nose grows red at the tip and profound emotion tears across her face. "I really missed you this last week."

I clear my throat and shift in my seat. I'm no good at heartfelt moments, but for her, I'll give it a shot. It's the least I can do. Reaching down deep, I hunt for the right words and lay them out between us.

"Listen, Annie. I want you to know that it was wrong of me to shut you out like I did. I hate myself for pushing you away over something that is important and life changing for you. If anything, you needed my support, and I was too self-absorbed to set my own insecurities aside and be there for you.

"I know an apology will never be enough, but it's all I've got, and I hope you'll accept it."

She smiles sweetly. It's the only kind she's ever had. Her eyes well with tears an instant before they start falling down her now ruddy cheeks. "You're in my apartment, aren't you?"

Throwing herself across the single cushion dividing us, she pulls me into a choking hug. I guess that's her way of telling me that I'm forgiven. I hug her back fiercely and take a relieved breath, because I was so close to losing this person that I need in my life.

Several minutes have passed by the time she pulls away and settles back on her side of the sofa. We both have to wipe our cheeks and touch up the makeup that has spread beneath our eyes, but it feels as though a tremendous weight has been lifted off my chest.

"I was never mad at you, you know," Annie says as she wipes her nose with a tissue. "I understand why you were upset. I kind of hit you with the news out of nowhere and Jason is involved and…"

…and I have an extreme dislike for Jason. The words are left unspoken, but they don't have to be for me to understand her meaning.

She waves her hand in the air and rolls her eyes at the ceiling. "Anyway, there's nothing to forgive. You're my sister from another mother. We fight, we get angry with each other sometimes, but we'll always be sisters."

That's always been our motto. I don't know how I could have forgotten that, but I'm glad she reminded me. It means we'll always have each other's back. Even when we're alone, we'll never truly be alone, and that is a security in life that no amount of money can buy. "Right, well, I'm still happy we're okay."

"Me, too, J." She sits up, her expression lightening. A wide smile that shows all of her teeth emerges and when she speaks, her whole body is animated. "Oh, you have to see this." Getting up, she dances away.

I follow her into the single bedroom, and studiously ignore the queen-sized bed that sits unmade, as though she and Jason have just rolled out of it. That is not a picture I want in my head.

Annie directs my attention to an old wooden rocking chair in the corner of the room, nestled between the wall and long vanity dresser. It looks like a poster child for lead poisoning and is painted a pale yellow that's cracked and peeling...everywhere.

"I picked it up at the flea market the other day for a steal. I thought I would paint it blue or pink, and do that whole shabby chic thing with it, then put it in the baby's room. What do you think?"

I look at my friend, whose smile is positively lovely. Her shining blonde hair brushes the tops of her shoulders and she looks...happy. As much as I dislike the circumstances, I can't help joining her. The chair is in rough shape, but with a little work, I know she'll make it great. If anyone can do it, it's Annie.

"I think it's perfect. You could even make a little cushion to tie to the spindles, so your butt doesn't fall asleep when you sit in it," I add.

"That's a great idea," she says, clapping her hands together beneath her chin. Then she aims two fingers at me like a gun. "Hey, maybe you can come with me to pick out the fabric?"

My reply is instant. "Absolutely. We can make a day of it."

"Want to go right now?"

Her exuberance says I don't have much of a choice, so I nod just as eagerly. "What are we still standing here for? Let's go!"

We end up spending the rest of the day out shopping. By the time we make it back to her apartment, it's dusk. We made out well. Maybe a little too well. Both of our arms are loaded up to the elbow with goodies, and I help Annie carry the bags up the two flights of stairs, complaining the whole way about her only asking me along because she needed a pack mule. Her tinkling laughter carries through the hallway all the way to her door and is replaced by a warm smile when the door to her apartment swings open.

Jason is standing on the other side, his semi-muscled shoulders tensed and his cold stare trained on me. My good mood instantly evaporates. As he reaches out to take Annie's bags, he leans down and gives her a lingering kiss.

Giving them their privacy, I look away. Now that the mood is significantly subdued, it's time for me to leave. Jason holds the door and I shuffle inside, laying the rest of the bags on the dining room table.

"Okay, lady, I had fun today, but you wore me out," I tell Annie as I stretch my fingers and arms, which are marked with deep grooves and tinged a deep shade of red from holding the bags. "I'm going to head home and veg out on some Mafia Wives."

"Are you sure?" Annie looks disappointed as she returns my hug. "We're ordering pizza tonight. You're welcome to stay and eat dinner with us."

She means it, but one look at Jason and I know that invitation is one-sided. I wouldn't have accepted anyway. "No, thanks. I need to keep my figure up," I say, patting my flat stomach. "Eat an extra slice for me?"

"You know it. Hey," Annie says as she sees me to the door. "I know I already said it, but I think it bears repeating. If by the end of this class you're still hung up on this guy, you need to give him another chance. It's a tough situation, but it sounds like he really liked you."

I almost regret telling her what happened between me and Ransom. Almost. The fact is, she's good at dishing out advice, and I'd be stupid not to eat at her table. I take her words to heart, but I can't be sure what, if anything, I will do with them. Only time will tell. "I'll think about it."

I wave as I slip past Jason, flashing him a tight smile on my way out. He mumbles a very unenthusiastic goodbye and I hear the door click closed before I reach the top of the stairs.

What she sees in him, I don't know, but if she's happy, then I'm willing to pretend I'm happy, too. Lord knows, I'm great at lying. What must it be like, looking at life through a pair of rose-colored glasses? And where can I find a pair?

***

The last few weeks of the semester fly by. Between work and school and spending time with my friends, I hardly notice it. Keeping busy is the secret to maintaining any level of sanity, especially during the tough times life hands out.

That's how I got through my mother's passing: I threw myself into soccer and friends and adopting the role of daughter and homemaker. It's also how I got past my father's death. Before you know it, time has skated by you and wounds that used to ache are beginning to scab over.

Ransom has shown up at the club a few times. He's watched me dance, but I don't watch him. He's asked for me personally, but I decline. Then he left a number for me with Bernice—I assume, out of desperation—and even though I have no intention of calling it, it sits buried in my purse.

It's a small source of comfort to know that I could hear his voice anytime with just the push of a few buttons. It's also a big source of stress because each day that passes makes me wonder how much longer I can prevent myself from picking up the phone.

The problem has only grown deeper as my impending show approaches, and now that it's finally here, I find my hand searching for that scrap of paper. I won't call it, but I desperately want to. I spent a lot of time preparing myself for this night, but now that it's here, all of my insecurities are jumping to the forefront of my mind.

Is this how I want people to see me? Is it really worth taking my clothes off for? Does this cheapen me somehow? It's supposed to be art, that's what Mrs. Jackson said, but blending nude art with education somehow feels wrong.

But it's a paying gig, and that's what ultimately has me walking into that room Wednesday night.

There are easels set up in a circle around the edges of the room, creating a stage for the table placed dead center. It's draped with white fabric that I think was intended to make the space more inviting, when in reality it lends it a clinical feel. I hate it instantly and a voice inside my head whispers that it's not too late to turn around. I'm the only one here, so they would just assume I never showed up, right?

The idea is blown to hell when I turn to find Mrs. Jackson approaching. She's dressed in a long, flowing tie-dyed dress and she's pushing a cart stacked with paint, brushes, and other supplies. And she's looking right at me with a pleased smile. "Good, you're here. To be honest, I wasn't sure you'd show."

As I move to the side to give her room to pass, I feel my brows pull down.

Even though she hasn't seen my expression, she continues speaking. "You probably wouldn't know it from the level of cockiness in your fellow classmates, but there are a lot of cold feet at this school, especially the boys. They'll strip down and blaze a naked path through a football field on game day for a laugh, but they're shaking in their sneakers if you ask them to get naked and take a load off so a few people can draw a picture."

I laugh nervously as I set my purse down on a nearby table and follow her deeper into the room. She stops the cart midway and positions it near a large sink basin.

Before I forget, I fish the paper Ransom gave me from my pocket and hold it out. "I need you to fill this out. It's a questionnaire and proof that I was here."

She takes it, and unfolding the paper, gives it a once-over. "This is for your final project?"

"Yes, it is."

She nods and reaches over to drop it on top of her desk, sighing wistfully. "What I wouldn't have given to have such a cool assignment for my final exam when I was your age. I'll have it back to you at the end of class." Leaning back, she props herself on the edge of the desk, and her expression is all business. "Okay, here's the drill," she says as she eyes me. "I assume this is your first time?"

"Yes." That single word reveals the nerves currently creating a maelstrom inside my stomach.

Her smile is kind, but her words are frank. "You think you're nervous now? Just wait until my class shows up. That's the true test for everyone." Pointing to the table in the center of the room, she says, "That's your stage tonight. Once everyone is seated and ready to go, I'll have you start by lying down on your side, facing my desk."

Crap. I have to walk into a crowded room and get naked. I don't suppose she has a stripper pole that I can warm up on. "That's it? I just lie down and they draw me?"

"To start. The class is expected to draw three images tonight from three different angles. So we'll get you lying down facing one direction, then have you flip over so they can draw you from a new perspective, and we'll finish with a sitting portrait."

I gulp. "How long is the class again?"

"Only an hour, and don't worry, you'll survive," she says, her voice ringing with laughter. Clasping my shoulder, she looks me in the eye with utmost sincerity. "I'm sure you've heard this before, but everyone is nervous the first time. I can tell just standing here that you have a gorgeous figure and most important, you're confident in your looks. Don't let a little case of the nerves run you off. I am a firm believer that facing the things that strike fear in you is a great way to build character."

I'm sure she's right, but that doesn't dull the churning feeling gripping me right now. Retrieving a white fluffy robe from cabinet near her desk, Mrs. Jackson directs me to a room that looks to be a teacher's lounge that she claims all the models use and is completely secure. There are textbooks littering a small circular table at its center, and a short row of cabinets along the wall behind it that house an overlarge coffee maker, stacks of Styrofoam cups and stirrers, various creamers, and a microwave. It's exactly what I imagined a teacher's lounge to look like.

Glimpsing a mini fridge humming off to the side, I steal a bottle of water and gulp it down, hoping it will give me enough distraction to calm down.

Then I realize what a total mistake I just made, because I'll end up having to use the bathroom a dozen times, so I spend the next ten minutes in the adjacent bathroom trying to evacuate my bladder.

Twenty minutes later, and I am standing outside a closed door completely naked but for the robe clenched around me. The blue and cream speckled linoleum is cool under my bare feet. Through a long, rectangular window, I can see Mrs. Jackson lecturing her students. There's a mix of men and women, all roughly my age, seated on their stools in front of the canvasses they will be immortalizing my image on.

It strikes me all over again that I go to school with these people. If they didn't know me before, they will now. I'll be the-girl-who-took-her-clothes-off.

Before I can freak myself out more, Mrs. Jackson notices my presence and her burgundy painted lips split into a wide grin. She says something to the class, and they all turn their heads to look at me.

God, I should run now. But I don't.

Mrs. Jackson walks over and opens the door. "Come in, come in. We were just talking about you." She waves me inside with a flip of her hand, and I follow her into the room. My focus is on her back, on the way the fabric ripples like soft ocean waves with each step she takes. If I look up, I'll bolt. It's that simple.

"Please drop your robe and stretch out on the table," she directs.

My fingers tighten on the plush fabric for a brief instant before I shove it away. I climb onto the table, feeling the slight chill of the wood seep through thin cotton sheet against my buttocks. Turning onto my side, I allow Mrs. Jackson to manipulate my limbs how she wants them. My right arm stretches out, is bent at the elbow with my hand opened wide to support my head. My left arm is brought forward on the table to steady me. My legs, which are clamped tight together and stretched long, are separated. She brings one knee forward, and I tense as the air touches between my thighs.

My mind goes wild imagining what the students positioned directly south of me must see. What will they draw? Do they like what they see? Are they turned on, or just as embarrassed as I am? I may take off my clothes for a living, but that doesn't make me an exhibitionist. I don't enjoy showing off my body to anyone willing to look at it. At least, not in this context. Even in a strip club, there are boundaries, limitations.

After I am positioned just how Mrs. Jackson wants me, she leaves the circle, taking on the role of an observer. "Okay, class. As you know, you have twenty minutes to perform your first sketch. Try to capture the form as you see it. Focus on light and shadow and use it to create depth in the drawing. I will be walking around the room to take a peek at everyone's work. If you have a question for me, just raise your hand and I will come over. Clock starts now."

With the exception of the light scratching of pencils on canvas and the dull clack of Mrs. Jackson's pumps as she moves around the room, everything is silent. At first it makes me even more aware of all the eyes on me, but as the minutes tick by, I begin to relax and I find my thoughts drifting inward.

I'm in a nearly sleep-like state by the time we're halfway into the second pose, when I hear the knock on the door. It's a faint rap, and my gaze flicks up, following Mrs. Jackson's back as she walks over to answer it.

She opens the door a crack and sticks her head out—murmurs follow, the words unintelligible. Although curious, I retreat back into myself.

I know I shouldn't, but I've been using this time to reflect on my relationship with Ransom. Annie's suggestion is still fresh in my mind and with the end of class looming on the horizon, I've come to realize that I am not over him. Not in the slightest. Severing ties hasn't worked. Having to see him every day, in fact, has only made the distance worse.

Seeing but no touching. The detached way we speak to each other. The longing looks and denial that nothing is going on between us. All of it keeps the wounds fresh.

Without that clean break, it's impossible to close the door. Instead, the smallest look or spoken word sends it flying wide open again.

The memories are inescapable, and so is he.

That point is only solidified when Mrs. Jackson steps back and I see Ransom enter the room.

Twenty-One

My heart stops dead in my chest and my gaze skates down Ransom's body. He's dressed in simple black slacks and a pale pink button-down shirt, and I can't help drinking him. It's like he was plucked right out of my thoughts and dropped into the room just to torture me.

What is he doing here? I communicate the question with a firm look, one that Ransom returns with a cool, even face that reveals absolutely nothing.

Defiance. That's what I'm labeling that look. He knows this is the last place he should be, the last place I would want him to be, but he showed up anyway. Annie once said he was a man abusing his power, and I have to admit, right now I agree with her. I wonder what he told himself to defy all of his rules and risk being here tonight.

Mrs. Jackson is giving him a guided tour of her students' work, pointing to certain aspects that she finds notable. He nods and murmurs a reply at all the right times, but each time he looks away from me, his gaze returns a heartbeat later.

The more it happens, the more my insides flare with heat. It's a demanding ache that starts in my chest as a flicker of nerves and travels lower until it's a burning desire for so much more. He scans my body, and to the casual observer, it's a clinical assessment. Just a professor observing art in progress. To me, though, this is foreplay. Annie may have been right, but I find that I don't really mind.

He's teasing me with his constant looks. And that hint of a smile teasing his thick, firm lips? He slays me. I can't stop the memories of him looking at me like that when he was inside of me.

It's impossible to miss the desire in his eyes, just as it's impossible to deny the mounting need in my belly as he moves beyond my peripheral vision. Unable to see him, my breathing grows deeper, heavier, and I have to double my efforts to concentrate on maintaining my pose.

"She's doing very well," Mrs. Jackson comments, and my ears perk up.

"I can see that." Ransom's voice is soft and husky. Unobtrusive in the otherwise quiet room, but like a pin drop, I hear every word.

"If only all of my models were as poised as this one. I'm tempted to bribe her into dropping your class and joining mine." There's a teasing lilt to Mrs. Jackson's voice, but I suspect she's partially serious.

"The semester ends in two weeks, Celeste. You're free to scoop up whoever you want then."

"Indeed I will."

"Do you mind if I sit in on the rest of the class? I'd love to see the finished products."

"Absolutely," Mrs. Jackson says wholeheartedly. "You can have my chair if you'd like."

I want so badly to turn and look at him. I can feel Ransom's eyes on me, staring at the slope of my back, the curve of my butt. The place between my thighs that begs for his attention.

When Mrs. Jackson calls for the final round of sketches to begin, I stand on unsteady legs and try not to focus too much on the moisture pooled between my legs. A fact that becomes impossible to ignore when she draws up a chair and tells me to straddle it.

I'm facing Ransom this time, unable to escape from that penetrating gaze. With as much brazenness as I can muster, I ease down onto the hard wood and prop my arms on the back of the chair, folding them one over the other. The air touches my exposed clit, and with my thighs split open, I am painfully aware of how aroused I am.

Mrs. Jackson artfully arranges my hair over my shoulders, so it cascades down my back, and then she gives me a perfunctory nod, pleased with her work, and disappears to resume her walk around the room.

I am out of my element. Ransom's eyes study mine, his dark gaze narrowed slightly as if he recognizes this about me. I refuse to look away first. Confidence, that's the image I want to project. I'm also hoping that my actions will inform him that this thing between us isn't over. If there were any hope of ending things between us, it ended the moment he walked through that door.

As his eyes drop lower, lingering on my breasts, which have firmed in the air-conditioned room, I don't think that will be a problem. Ransom doesn't appear to have given up either. As his gaze lands at the gap created by the chair between my legs, I see his nostrils flare and his lips part and something inside me just…snaps.

Between one breath and the next, I have decided that I won't be leaving here tonight alone. I made a mistake when I sent him away, and now I fully intend to rectify the situation.

Despite the cool air skating down my spine from overhead, beads of perspiration form around my hairline and under my arms, making me feel damp all over. By the time the class ends and the robe is returned to me, my mouth feels like I've stuffed it with cotton balls. It doesn't matter that I downed an entire bottle of water before coming in here. I'm dehydrated, and it's all Ransom's fault.

He makes me crazy. Needy. Desperate.

I'm directed back to the teacher's lounge, where I change back into my street clothes. When I return the robe to Mrs. Jackson, Ransom is nowhere to be seen.

My shoulders drop and my mood deflates. I can't deny that I am disappointed by this. I had plans. Plans that involved signaling him to meet me outside. Where the dark sky would provide the perfect backdrop for our reunion. Was I confident that I would win him back? Not even remotely, but sometimes a girl has to lie to herself to find the courage she needs to press forward.

"You did great tonight," Mrs. Jackson praises as she signs my form and hands it back. Her golden eyes twinkle as she looks up at me from behind her desk. "How did you enjoy the experience?"

I feel my cheeks heat as I think about just how much I enjoyed it once Ransom walked in. "It was different. Once I relaxed, it wasn't too bad."

"Good, then I hope you'll consider coming back. I could always use a few more willing victims."

I shake her hand, not giving her a response, and she wishes me a good evening.

Despite the disappointment I feel, I walk out of the building with my head held high. Tonight I feel like I've overcome something. I don't know what it is, but I feel good, and I'm glad that I chose to see it through.

The path I take is winding and framed by arching utility lights which create a swath of salmon colored light that's a little hard on the eyes. Because it's after dark, and I am alone but for a few people off in the distance, the campus takes on an eerie atmosphere. I can almost imagine a serial killer lurking in the shadows.

Kicking up my pace, I hurry to reach the nearly vacant parking lot. My car is one of a handful left, and as I notice the figure standing in wait, my heart skips a beat and my steps falter.

Until I realize who it is.

My heart skips before redoubling its effort and my blood quickens, pounding in my ears as I close the distance between us. When he hears my footsteps approaching, his dark head lifts and he steps into the light.

"Ransom." My voice is breathy, relieved and excited and so many things I can't begin to name, and as he meets me halfway and I leap into his waiting arms, into his fervent kiss, everything seems to click into place.

This is where I want to be. Where I should have been all along. None of the problems that faced us are gone, yet they cease to matter anymore. I wrap my arms and legs around his sturdy frame and kiss him with abandon. There is no care for the world around us. At this moment, only the two of us exist.

"You taste so good," Ransom says against my mouth. His hands cup my butt, squeezing the soft globes and pressing me against his erection.

I lick his lips, wanting to taste him everywhere. There is no time to think, only act, and as I am the one driving this train, I issue the directions. "Keys. In my purse." That's all the information I give him, but being the intelligent man he is, Ransom doesn't need anything more.

In a matter of moments, he has the door open and is shoving our entwined bodies into the spacious backseat of my Camry. My hands dive between our heaving bodies and begin working on his belt as he grasps both halves of my collared polo. With a vicious yank, the fabric tears easily from collar to belly button.

I look at him with what I imagine to be a mix of horror, anger, and lust. The latter emotion wins out. "That's just about the hottest thing I have ever witnessed."

He grins, and in the dark, it makes him look sinister. I like it. No, scratch that. I fucking love that.

My hands can't move fast enough. Once his belt is undone, I shimmy the loose fabric over his firm ass. His cock springs out, standing like an arrow pointing to home base.

The throbbing between my legs increases and I whimper and arch my back as Ransom licks my nipples through my lacy bra. His hands slip between the stretchy waistband on my pants and guide them over my hips along with my underwear. When the material bunches up at my knees, he doesn't stop to remove my shoes so he can finish the task.

No. Ransom is too impatient for that.

Instead, he lifts both legs up setting them on his right shoulder, ankles crossed, and leans forward, crushing my knees to my chest. The toes of my Keds scrape the fabric of the car's ceiling as he gets into position.

Like this, our faces are only inches apart and with the way the light from the parking lot shines through the back window, all I see is him.

He's all I ever see.

His cockhead presses into me, and I struggle for breath as I look into his eyes. "You feel it too don't you, Joe? You feel that tightness in your chest. The kind that steals your breath and makes you feel like you might die even as everything in your world feels like it's finally fallen into place." His voice is thick and raspy, causing tendrils of heat to coil between my legs where his cock threatens to split me wide open.

"This is where I belong, Josephine. Between your silky thighs, buried so deep that you feel me inside your chest. That's where I live, Joe, right here." His hot palm covers the space between my breasts, directly over my pounding heart. "Don't try to send me away again, because I'm not leaving."

Hot tears leak from the corners of my eyes and spill into the hair at my temples. My reply is simple. "I won't." Two words, and it's done. We're together again. Sometimes that's all it takes.

My lungs constrict as his hips surge forward. My eyes burn as he stretches me, making good on his promise—I feel him, all the way to my heart.

***

Sometime later, I rouse from the light sleep I've fallen into. The windows are fogged up and the air inside the car is cold but heavy. My skin prickles with goosebumps, the fine hairs on my arms standing on end. I burrow deeper into Ransom's arms, trying to soak up as much of his heat as I can. Like all men, he's a furnace, almost too hot to touch, but too tempting to stay away. My fingers travel across his chest, playing with the fine hairs that dust it.

"Why did you stick around?" The question spills from my mouth before it's a conscious thought.

His answer is a long time coming. Covering my hand with his, he says, "How could I not? You're special to me, Joesphine. You give me something I haven't had in a long time. Hell, I'm not sure I've ever had it, but it feels right."

"What's that?" I ask, angling my head back to look at him.

He tilts his head down and kisses my mouth. "Feelings, Joe. You make me feel things I know I shouldn't, but that I can't stop. Believe me, I've tried."

I know what he means. Although, I don't think either of us has really tried all that hard. Lust—it's one of the deadliest sins. "Feelings don't always make sense."

"I don't think they're supposed to." He pauses, his hand tightening around mine. "I want you to come back to my place, spend the night."

"I thought…" Surprised, my words trail off. It feels like we're in a bubble right now. A bubble that's in danger of bursting if I don't choose my words carefully.

"That I didn't want you there," Ransom finishes for me, and I nod. Easing me off of him, he sits up and rakes a hand through his damp hair. Drawing my knees up to my chest, I huddle into myself as I wait for him to continue.

Sex looks good on him. His skin is flushed, his lips a deeper shade of red and plumped from my kisses, and his clothes are rumpled and twisted in a way that makes me want to ravage him all over again.

Turning his head, Ransom pins me with a look. "It's not that I didn't want you there. I just didn't think it was a good idea."

"And now you do? Ransom, nothing's changed. I'll still be your student in the morning."

Lying back against the seat, he drops his head back and stares up at the stars through the foggy glass. The position highlights the corded muscles lining the sides of his neck and the Adam's apple that moves up and down enticingly with each swallow.

"I thought about what you said. Being together presents some risks, but being apart?" His head rolls to the side and his dark eyes find mine. "I can find a job anywhere, Joe, but there's never going to be another you."

My lungs constrict, making it difficult to breathe properly. I don't think anyone has ever spoken anything as beautiful as that to me before.

"I don't know what this is between us is or where it's headed," he continues, his gaze focused overhead. "There's already a black mark on our record, and for all I know, we'll change our mind again in the morning, or maybe a week from now or a month. What I do know is that I like this"— he gestures between us—"I like how I feel when we're together. Life is too short to miss out on the things that make us feel good, make us feel *alive*, and I feel so alive with you."

"And if someone does find out that we're together, what then? Are you going to be okay if you lose your job over me?"

"We'll cross that bridge if we have to." He reaches out and takes my hand, pulling me over to cover his body with mine. Cupping the back of my head, he holds me against his chest, and when he speaks, I feel the warmth of his breath in my hair. "The only thing that matters right now is this, right here, right now."

I wiggle closer, listening to the steady beat of his heart beneath my ear. This is one of those rare, perfect moments in time that life occasionally hands out. It would be so easy to just give into it and enjoy it for what it is, but I've experienced them a couple times before. I know not to trust them. There is such a thing as something being too perfect, too right. When all the pieces of the puzzle seem to be in place, that's the time to sit up and pay attention.

I can feel it in the air, like the kind of calm that comes before a tornado touches down and destroys everything. I don't know what form it's going to take, but I know one thing for sure.

A storm is coming.

Twenty-Two

After a couple more rounds of lovemaking, Ransom is out. He snores. Soft, whispers of sound that rumbles subtly in his chest. I'm in his bed, in his apartment, folded up in his arms, and I can't fall asleep. It should be the simplest thing to do, but every time I try, my eyes flip open as if they're spring loaded.

It could be because I am used to keeping late hours at the club, or because my mind is churning over everything that happened tonight and the inability to predict what lies ahead of us tomorrow. But my money is on what's going on beyond the bedroom because, about an hour ago, I heard someone enter the apartment.

They came in through the front door, their keys clanking against a hard surface, suggesting to me that whoever it is isn't an intruder. But who is it? A roommate? Ransom never mentioned having one, but then again, there are still a lot of things I don't know about the man whose bed I'm sharing.

Curiosity picks away at my patience. I want to go investigate, but I don't dare. Do I? It's not my place. How will Ransom and this other person respond to my snooping around? Besides, Ransom's arms around my waist are tethering me to him and the bed and there's no way in hell I'll be able to slip free without waking him.

I don't know how much time I spend lying there, listening to this mystery person move around the apartment. I track their footsteps from the front of the apartment, where they spend some time in the kitchen making all kinds of muffled racket that I'd probably never notice if I had already been asleep.

The television plays on low for a time, and then the footsteps carry down the hall, past the bedroom door, and into the bathroom. I tense as I listen to every minute sound—running water in the sink, the hiss of the shower, the flushing of a toilet. All normal things people do to get ready for bed. I listen until my eyelids grow heavy—the constant rush of the water serving as a lullaby.

I finally fall asleep after everything goes quiet and the footsteps disappear down the end of the hall where a door, that had been closed when we arrived, opens and shuts again.

Hours later, when the alarm goes off, I feel like someone has piled a load of bricks on my chest and legs and taped my eyelids shut. I moan my refusal to get up and turn over, burying my head beneath the pillow. Ransom's body covers mine from behind, his soft chuckle in my ear as he nuzzles me making me squirm.

"Time to get up. Don't want to be late for school," he taunts.

"I'm not going today. Tell them I'm sick."

Hands wandering down my naked body, he kisses the back of my neck. "Sorry, but sexual exhaustion is no excuse to slack on your education, young lady."

"Please," I whine as he rolls me over and positions himself between my slack thighs. He looks up at me, a wicked smile twisting his lips up at the corners.

"Nope, but I know something that will wake you up."

"Ransom!" I gasp and my fingers delve into his hair as his mouth forms a seal over my clit. His tongue flicks back and forth, and the hands cupping my butt lift my hips, pulling me closer so he can bury his face in me.

His fingers penetrate my opening as he continues to lap at me, and my hips buck uncontrollably as he brings me to the fastest climax I've ever had. I lay there, boneless and breathless for what feels like an eternity. I used to think that orgasms were a rare phenomenon, but Ransom's quickly proving that theory wrong.

When I finally manage the strength to open my eyes, Ransom is pulling on a pair of jeans.

Leaning over me, he sucks my bottom lip into his mouth and releases it with a smack. His dark eyes dance with mirth as he pulls away and backs toward the door. "I'm going to start breakfast. Join me when you can walk again."

Damn him, that cocky bastard. When he's gone, I stare up at the ceiling wondering what I've gotten myself into. My mind spirals down a dangerous path of what-if scenarios until even I am sick of hearing the insecure thoughts running around in my head. Last night, when I got into the backseat of my car with him, I decided that there was no more running from this. No more indecisive bullshit. If we're going to make an honest go of it, then I can't walk away at the first bump to appear in the road.

Locating Ransom's discarded shirt on the floor, I slip it on and fasten enough buttons to look presentable, and then gather my clothes up. A quick shower and then breakfast, that's the plan.

The heavenly smell of bacon sizzling in the pan hits me when I step out of the room, but despite my stomach's demand for sustenance, I head in the opposite direction.

The second bedroom's door at the end of the hall is still closed, so I guess whoever Ransom rooms with is sleeping, which makes sense. They came in extremely late last night. I wonder what the story is. If they're friends or family. Maybe an ex.

That thought sets me on edge, and I shake it off before I decide to march in there and find out who this person is. All I know is that it had better not be an ex-girlfriend. God, what if it's Red?

Right, I need to stay focused and think rationally, and a warm shower is just the ticket.

The door to the bathroom stands partway open. I push it aside...and jump back with a startled squeak.

Ransom stands in front of the sink, a black towel slung low around his hips. Even though he scared the tar out of me, I quickly recover as I let the vision of him nearly naked set in.

Water droplets cover the span of his wide shoulders, occasionally gliding down the deep crevasse of his spine to soak into the plush fabric hiding one of my favorite parts to ogle. He's in the process of shaving, which is a shame, because I rather enjoy the feel of his stubble scratching my skin when he kisses me.

His eyes leap to mine in the mirror as I stand in the doorway, and the razor stops mid-stroke. A small bead of crimson appears on his chin and is captured by droplets of water, which collect and begin running in a single rivulet of red down his neck.

Slowly, he lowers his arm, the razor hanging loosely in his hand. "What are you doing here?"

His tone is sharp and commanding, his black eyes filled with dangerous intent, and the change in him is such a shock that my head jerks back.

"I'm sorry. I was going to grab a quick shower. I didn't think you'd mind." My words are small, full of apprehension. I don't understand why he'd be upset with me. Have I crossed some invisible boundary?

I hitch my thumb over my shoulder. "I thought you were cooking breakfast?"

His eyes narrow a fraction more as his reflection continues to glare at me. Lowering his head, he dips the razor into the basin of murky water and swishes it around. Then, he pulls the plug. I stand there and watch him finish his routine, carefully replacing the razor in a custom silver hanger and splashing on a clean smelling aftershave.

When he is finished, he turns to fully face me, covering the two steps that separate us and crowds the doorway with his large body. I look up into his dark eyes, feeling dwarfed, feeling vulnerable.

I realize with a note of apprehension that this isn't the man who brought me to orgasm this morning and kissed me goodbye so he could go make me breakfast. The man, who stands before me now, is cold and menacing. I feel as if I've just walked into a lion's den at feeding time. I feel exposed, unwelcome, in danger.

It's the exact same feeling I felt every time we met in his hotel room.

"What's wrong? Did I do something?"

He studies me with his perfect features, with this perfect calm that only serves to make me feel even more unsteady like there's not enough oxygen in the room.

"How did you get into my apartment?"

I'm confused by the question. "Are you serious?" I tilt my head to see if there is any hint of teasing in his eyes, but he's completely unmoved. "You brought me here last night. I slept in your bed." Nothing. I'm staring at a blank wall. "Did you fall and hit your head in the shower or something?"

The pulse in his jaw ticks wildly. "Or something." Securing the towel with one hand, he takes my arm in the other and moves me out of his way as he steps out of the bathroom. Then, he forcibly guides me down to the end of the hall where it opens into a great room comprised of the living and dining rooms and a spacious kitchen.

As we continue moving forward, I catch movement ahead. All I can see is a pair of blue jean clad legs moving around, and I assume that it's his roommate who's taken to cooking us breakfast—a meal I have decided not to stick around for.

Something is up with Ransom, and I know I told myself that I wouldn't run at the first bump in the road, but he's acting strange. Well, stranger than usual. I don't know if he suffers from a split personality disorder, if he's bipolar, or if he really did take a nasty fall in the shower this morning, but I'm not comfortable with the current situation. I need to go home, collect my thoughts, and ruminate over them a while.

"I found this wandering around in the hall," Ransom growls, jerking me in front of him as we enter the circle of cabinets that define the kitchen. "Care to explain to me what she's doing here?"

I frown, my mouth parting on a protest that sticks in my throat the moment the roommate turns from the stove.

"Holy…shit. There are two of you."

I've just stepped into the *Twilight Zone*. An exact replica of Ransom stands before me, only this one is dressed exactly the way the Ransom who left the bedroom this morning looked. A quick appraisal tells me that those are indeed the same low-slung jeans I saw him leave the room in.

Looking up at Ransom Number Two, I see all the same details from the curve of his lips to the slope of his jaw, to the high, round cheekbones. All of it is the same.

"Damn," Ransom Number One says. "I'm sorry. I meant to tell you earlier."

"Meant to tell me what exactly?" My body feels like it's been stuck in one of those paint mixing machines at Home Depot. I'm trembling and I can't seem to stop. Stepping to the side, Ransom Number Two's hand falls away, and I wrap my arms around myself.

Ransom Number One wears this goofy smile, like he thinks all of this is one giant joke. Well, I don't find any of this funny.

He walks over and puts his arm around my shoulder, tucking me against his chest and kissing the top of my head. The gesture would be soothing if I wasn't so damn confused. And then he says, "Joe, this is my brother, Rebel. We're identical twins."

Twenty-Three

The puzzle pieces finally click into place. The scene they create makes total sense now. Ransom has a brother. An identical brother. As we stand in the kitchen looking at one another, it dawns on me just how embarrassing this situation is.

"God," I say, hiding my face behind my hands. "I totally walked in on you in the bathroom."

Rebel maintains that stern frown, and I think he must be a real ass if he can't forgive an honest mistake. If he didn't want anyone to walk in on him, then he should have closed the damn door.

"Don't worry about it, babe," Ransom said cheerily. "Rebel's not exactly the shy type."

Rebel's hateful stare hasn't left me for a second, and when Ransom leaves my side to tend to the bacon, I scoot a little closer to him and farther away from his brother. Supposedly, everyone has an evil twin out there somewhere. Rebel must be Ransom's, I decide. Even his name seems to suggest it.

"Don't worry," Rebel says, his voice a deep, dark rasp. "It's nothing she hasn't seen before. Right....*Joe*?"

The way he says my name, like he's testing out the feel of it on his tongue, is disturbing. Oddly, I feel my body responding to the low timber of it as if his voice is calling to me on a deeper, more intimate level. It must be the resemblance. Or, rather, the effect of looking at the exact same image of the man who drives me crazy.

Ransom shoots his brother a condemning look over his shoulder and turns off the stove. "Stop trying to make my girlfriend feel uncomfortable, Rebel. I'm sure it's a pretty big shock to find out I have a doppelganger before she's had her morning cup of coffee."

"Imagine what a shock it must be for me, then, to see the woman I've been screwing these last few weeks dressed in my brother's shirt this morning."

Everything just stops. Time, breath, heartbeats. My head snaps up at the same time as Ransom's. He looks at me and then at his brother

230 | DANCE FOR ME

as if he's insane. Which he is because there is no way in hell I've slept with this man.

No way.

Is there?

I study both men again. They're exactly the same, every single detail. But, as they begin to argue, I start to realize that there are some differences. For instance, Ransom's voice is smoother, even when he's angry. Whereas Rebel's is a husky growl, no matter his mood.

That's the deciding factor. I'd thought the puzzle had finally clicked together? I was wrong. So very wrong.

What I didn't realize until this very moment was that a piece was missing—the one crucial piece of the puzzle responsible for pulling it all together in a nice, neat package.

Suddenly, the differences I'd recognized in Ransom are making sense. Perfect sense. All those times at the hotel and the club, when he'd been too rough, demanding, and callous compared to when I'd see him at the university, where he was subdued, softer, and more agreeable. When he'd made love to me and actually tended to my needs for once, instead of only worrying about his own.

Ransom wasn't always Ransom.

He was also Rebel.

Twins. Identical twins.

I'd been sleeping with two men.

Brothers.

My blood runs cold. Falling back, my hip bangs against the counter, but the impact is nothing against the heavy cloud of confusion, hurt, and betrayal that's slowly choking the air from my lungs.

Noticing the panic written on my face, the yelling stops and Ransom reaches for me. I move out of the way, refusing contact.

I don't want anyone touching me, least of all him. Them. Fuck! My head is spinning. I feel like I'm on a tilt-o-whirl, everything around me reduced to a blur of indistinct shapes and colors. My emotions are a mess of confusion, humiliation, and abject horror.

How could this have happened? How could I not have known?

"Joe, are you okay?" Ransom's concerned voice comes from a distance, and the feel of his hand on my arm is ethereal. A lined brown leather recliner enters my vision and I feel my legs buckle beneath me as I'm pushed into it.

Ransom kneels down in front of me and I see him, but I'm not sure if this is a dream or reality anymore. Any minute, I'm hoping I'll wake up still wrapped in his arms and all of this will have been some twisted joke my brain cooked up.

"She's in shock," Ransom says, and another set of bare feet, feet that I recognize, enter my vision.

"It's not every day that you find out you've been screwing brothers. The question is, do you think she knew what she was doing?"

"Does this look like a reaction that someone who knew what they were doing would have?" Ransom answers angrily.

"Women play games. You know this as well as I do, brother."

"Well, she's not." Cupping my face in his hands, Ransom leans closer, looking me in the eyes. "I'm sorry, baby. I should have told you sooner. I should have…" His voice strangles and he squeezes his eyes shut and his head droops on his shoulders.

I don't know what he's apologizing for. It's me who messed up. I couldn't tell the difference. Or maybe I didn't want to. Both of them have fulfilled a need in me. But what have I done for them, besides creating a rift in their relationship.

"When did you start seeing her?" Ransom's voice is quiet, filled with a mixture of regret and worry.

"The beginning of summer, nine months ago. It was right after I returned from New York."

There is something in Rebel's voice that hints at a deeper story, but Ransom speaks up. "Nine months," he murmurs. He looks up at me again, his dark eyes hardening. "That explains a lot."

Yes, it does. He stands, turns away, and begins pacing.

"Maybe we should sit down together and compare notes," Rebel drawls, and from the look on his face, I get the impression that in his anger, he's looking to drum up trouble. "I wonder who she's more responsive to, you or me."

"This isn't a fucking contest!" Ransom shouts. It's enough to shock my system, and I shoot to my feet, claiming their attention.

"I'm not staying here for this." I need to leave. Get out of here. Go home where things are simple and there isn't a war ready to break out in front of me. Right now, I feel like someone is playing a joke on me. Is Annie in a back room somewhere, ready to pop out and tell me I've been *Punked?* There's no sign of Ashton Kutcher or a camera crew anywhere, so I have to assume that this is my life. I'm a stripper and a whore and a liar and it's all finally caught up with me.

I grab my clothes from where I left them—in a pile on the hallway floor. The bathroom is right there, so I lock myself inside and tear Ransom's shirt over my head. I am dressed in a matter of seconds, but it's trying to dial the phone with shaky fingers that holds me up. When I finally manage to type the number in without making any mistakes, I cry with relief.

Annie answers on the second ring. "Joe?" I sniffle, and her voice fills with concern and a touch of panic at not knowing what's wrong, but I don't have time to explain.

I give her the address and ask her to hurry. She doesn't ask questions, but I know they'll come in time.

Drawing in a steeling breath, I force myself to leave the room, and make a beeline for the exit. Ransom and Rebel are facing off in the living room, and I bypass them, hoping to go unnoticed. I get caught up fumbling with the multitude of locks, cursing and on the verge of tears, when Ransom's hand stops me. The heat of his skin on mine is a comfort I can't afford to fall into.

"Don't try to stop me," I snarl, yanking my hand away.

His expression is pained. "I wasn't going to. But if you wait a minute, I'll call you a cab."

I stay stuck in his haunted gaze long enough to drown before self-preservation kicks in and I force myself to break away. "Annie is on her way."

He nods solemnly and then reaches past me to turn one of the locks. The door creaks as it swings open and the fresh slice of air that leaks in makes my lungs inflate as if they're starving for oxygen.

"We'll talk soon," he promises me. My nod is automatic and before any more words can be exchanged, I escape through the door.

This time, I'm the one walking away.

It should make me feel strong, empowered. But the only thing I feel is the heavy weight of sadness that has settled on my shoulders.

Annie is waiting in her car, parked along the curb outside the building. Her eyes widen when she sees me, and I know I must look like shit. She doesn't comment as I climb into the passenger seat, only pausing long enough to ask if I'm okay.

My answer is simple, my voice dead, even to my ears. "No, but I will be."

Whatever happens tomorrow or the next day, I will be okay…because I have to be. I am Josephine Hart, and I was built to stand on my own.

To be continued…

ABOUT THE AUTHOR

USA Today Bestselling author J.C. Valentine is the alter-ego of Brandi Salazar, whose enjoyment of tales of romance spurred her to branch out and create her own.

She lives in the Northwest with her husband, their wild children, and far too many pets. As a university student, she studies literature, which goes well with her dream of becoming an editor. Brandi entertains a number of hobbies including reading and photography, but her first love is writing fiction-in all its forms. Connect with JC on Facebook!

Made in the USA
Lexington, KY
24 September 2015